Mallory and Mary Ann Take New York

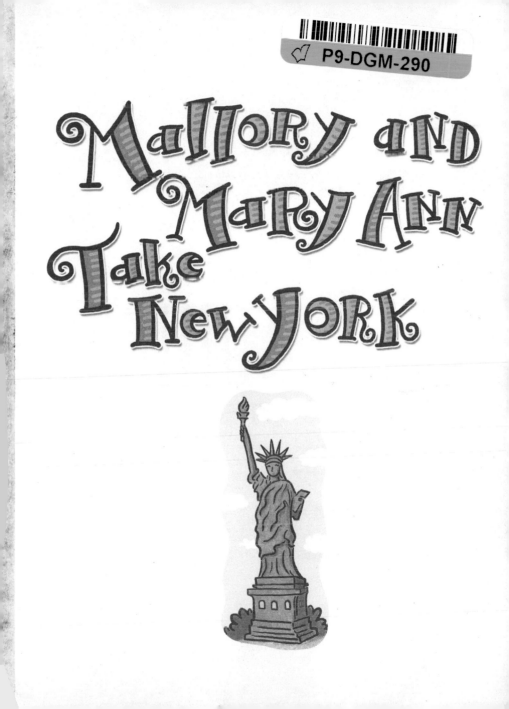

To Albert,
With all my love,
—Laurie

For little Juliette, my fashion princess
and best shopping buddy
—J.K.

Mallory and Mary Ann Take New York

by Laurie Friedman

illustrations by Jennifer Kalis

MINNEAPOLIS

CONTENTS

A WORD FROM MALLORY

My name is Mallory McDonald, like the restaurant but no relation. Age ten and a half.

Even though I'm only ten and a half, I've spent a lot of time, especially lately, thinking about what I want to be when I grow up.

I'll get to the "especially lately" part in a minute, but first, I want to talk about what I want to be when I grow up.

I'll start by telling you what I don't want to be.

I don't want to be a truck driver or a dermatologist (that's a doctor in charge of getting rid of pimples—ew). I also don't want to be a professional ice-skater (I'm terrible at ice-skating), a math teacher (I'm also terrible at math), or a zookeeper. The only animal I want to take care of is my cat, Cheeseburger.

I DO want to be an ice-cream scooper, a hairdresser, an astronaut, or a movie star. But there's something I want to be even more than all those things. I would LOVE to be a fashion designer.

I've been thinking a lot lately about being a fashion designer. (Remember how I said I would talk about the "especially lately" part later?)

The reason is that my favorite TV show, hosted by my favorite TV hostess, Fashion Fran, is about to have a fashion design contest for kids. I don't know a lot about the contest yet. But after today, I'll know a whole lot more.

Fashion Fran is going to announce the details of her contest on this afternoon's episode. My best friend, Mary Ann, and I have been waiting forever to find out what this contest is all about. The good news is we don't have to wait much longer.

Fashion Fran starts soon!

And we can hardly wait!

A CONTEST

"Hurry up! Fran is on in five!" I say into the phone.

"Get the popcorn and lemonade ready," Mary Ann says back. "I'll be right over with pens and paper."

One of the best parts about living next door to my best friend is that it doesn't take long to get to each other's houses. Mary Ann is on my couch before I even get there with the snacks.

Fashion Fran is about to announce the details of her fashion design contest that she has been talking about for weeks.

I turn on the TV and settle in next to Mary Ann.

She takes a sip of her lemonade. "I don't think I can wait another second," she says.

I shake my head. I agree completely. Fran announced the contest a few weeks ago, but it feels like it has taken months for it to officially begin. And today's the day. I can't wait to find out what it's all about.

As the music we've been listening to every afternoon for as long as I can remember starts to play, Mary Ann and I squeal.

Like always, we count down with the announcer as we wait for Fran to appear on the screen. "The moment we've been waiting for is finally here!" I say.

But before we get to enjoy it, my brother, Max, walks into the room.
He grabs the remote and changes the channel.

"I want to see the sports scores," he says.

Mary Ann and I both fly off the couch at the same time. So does the bowl of popcorn. My brother is usually faster than I am, but today I grab the remote out of his hand before he can stop me.

"Are you crazy?!?" I shout at Max. "Mary Ann and I have a V.I.S. to watch."

Max looks at me like he has no idea what I'm talking about, so I explain. "V.I.S. is short for *Very Important Show*." I tell him that Fashion Fran is having a design contest. "We're going to find out all of the details today!"

Now Max looks at me like I'm the one

who is crazy. "And you and Birdbrain actually think you can win?"

I wave my hand at Max to make him stop talking.

A. I don't like when he calls my best friend Birdbrain.

B. His question is ridiculous. We have as good a chance as anybody.

C. I don't have time to answer anyway. Fran is starting to talk.

Mary Ann and I both put our fingers to our lips and make a *shhh!* sound. But Max is already leaving. Mary Ann and I turn our attention to the TV.

"Fashionable viewers, welcome to a very special episode of the show." Fran smiles at the camera. She pats down her already smooth hair. Then she twirls so viewers can see what she's wearing.

"I love her sparkly sweater," I say.

"And her lace skirt," says Mary Ann.

We both shake our heads. One thing Mary Ann and I have always agreed on is that Fran is very fashionable.

The camera pans over the audience. It is filled with happy faces. "Can you even imagine what it would be like to be there?" I ask Mary Ann.

Mary Ann squeezes my arm.

It has always been our dream to be on her show together. But it is hard to imagine that ever happening. We watch as Fran keeps talking. "I'm sure you are all

anxious to hear about the design contest,"
says Fran. "But first, I want to tell you a
little bit about how I started as a fashion
designer."

I turn up the volume. I know Mary Ann
wants to hear this as much as I do.

Fran tells viewers how she loved playing
with fabrics and designing outfits when
she was a little girl. The camera cuts
to pictures of ten-year-old Fran using a
miniature sewing machine she says her
grandmother gave her.

"I have been sewing and designing ever
since." Fran smiles into the camera. "Now,
it is your turn."

"The contest is simple," says Fran.
"Design your dream outfit, your most
perfect, fashionable ensemble, on one
sheet of 8½ by 11 paper. Please use pencils
and colored pencils only. Send your design

to my studio in New York, addressed to Design Your Dream Outfit Contest."

A New York City address flashes on the front of the screen.

"Write that down," I say to Mary Ann.

Mary Ann starts writing.

Fran keeps talking. "You have three weeks to submit your design. I will personally look at each and every one that comes in." Lights twinkle on the screen behind Fran. She smiles into the camera. "And when we come back, I'll announce the prize for winning the Design Your Dream Outfit contest."

The TV cuts to a commercial.

"I can't wait to start designing," says Mary Ann. "Me too," I say to my best friend. My head starts filling up with ideas. I can already picture the dream outfits Mary Ann and I are going to design.

I'm really excited to design my dream outfit. But I'm even more excited to find out what you get if you win the contest.

When Fran returns, the lights twinkle again. "Now, the moment you have all been waiting for." A drum rolls in the background.

I squeeze Mary Ann's hand as Fran starts talking.

Fran raises an eyebrow and grins. "Viewers, I will choose the winning design. Then our seamstresses will sew it, creating a real dream outfit from the design." Fran pauses like what she's about to say next is the most exciting thing she has said so far. Mary Ann and I lean in toward the TV.

"The winner will receive an all-expenses-paid trip for four to New York City . . . AND a chance to appear on my show and model the winning design!"

When Fran says that, Mary Ann starts bouncing up and down on the couch. I'm starting to feel couch-sick. It's the same thing as seasick, except it happens when you're on a couch that is moving instead of a boat.

"Wow! Wow! Wow!" screams Mary Ann. "All we have to do is win the contest, and we get to go to New York City and model our outfits on the *Fashion Fran* show. We're going on *Fashion Fran*!"

I look at Mary Ann. I've never seen her so bouncy. I'm excited too, but I'm not sure why she's so bouncy. I'm also not sure why she used the word "we."

I put my hand on her arm and she stops moving. "Didn't you hear Fran?" I say. "She didn't say *"winners,"* she said *"winner."*

I wait for what I said to sink in, but it doesn't. Mary Ann waves at me like she's heard enough. She points to the screen. Fran is starting to talk again.

She holds up a sketch pad and a pencil.

"You design it. Our seamstresses sew it. One lucky winner will model her design on the show." Fran smiles. "This contest is only open for the next three weeks. So get busy drawing your dream outfit. I know there's a fashion designer in all of you."

Fran blows a kiss and waves. "That's it for today. See you tomorrow with more of the latest, greatest finds in the world of fashion."

The camera cuts to another commercial.

"*One lucky winner*" keeps spinning through my head. What was supposed to be the most exciting episode ever just turned into the worst episode ever. "What are we going to do?" I ask Mary Ann.

Mary Ann looks at me funny. "About what?"

Sometimes I wonder what goes on in Mary Ann's brain.

Is it working?

Mary Ann's brain

"Only one person gets to go on Fran's show. And there are two of us."

Mary Ann takes a deep *give-me-a-minute-to-think-about-this* breath. "It's simple," she says. "All we have to do is make a pinky swear. If one of us wins, we'll figure out a way to both go on the show."

She holds up her pinky like she's waiting for me to hook mine around hers.

I look at her. "How are we going to do that?"

Mary Ann shakes her head like now I'm the one who doesn't get it. "We need to stop talking and start promising!"

I shake my head. "I don't see how . . ."

I was going to say that I don't see how we could figure out something as big as both getting on the show, but Mary Ann stops me. She hooks my pinky in hers and shakes them up and down.

"Mallory, don't worry," she says. "Everything will work out fine. It always does when we make a pinky swear."

I nod. I try to imagine Mary Ann and me in New York. Seeing the sights. Modeling on the *Fashion Fran* show. But it's hard.

I know we made a pinky swear. But this time, I'm just not sure that's going to make everything work out.

CRUNCH TIME

I don't know why I was so worried about what happens if one of us wins the Design Your Dream Outfit contest. So far, it doesn't look like either one of us is going to win this contest.

It has been exactly two weeks and four days since Fashion Fran announced her Design Your Dream Outfit contest. For the last two weeks and four days, I have been designing outfits and Mary

Ann has been designing outfits.

We have been working on our designs every afternoon after school and on the weekends. We've hardly left my room.

The problem is . . . so far, none of our outfits look very dreamy.

Now it's crunch time. We only have three days to go before the contest is over.

I rip a sheet of paper out of the sketch pad I've been drawing in and crumple it into a ball. I toss it toward the trash can next to my desk. It misses and lands on my floor, next to the large pile of other wadded-up papers already on my floor.

Mary Ann leans back against the pillows on my bed and blows a piece of hair off her forehead. She tosses her sketch pad on the ground. "I give up."

"C'mon. We can't give up." I rub my head, which is what I do when I'm doing my most serious thinking. "We need to focus," I say.

Mary Ann snorts. "We've been focusing. I'm sick of focusing."

I pick up her sketch pad and hand it back to her. "Let's give it one more try. We just need to design the perfect outfit that we both would want to wear."

Mary Ann nods like she'll try, but she's not as into it as she was two weeks and four days ago.

I hand her a pencil, and we both flip to clean pages in our sketchbooks.

I really want to do a good job. I really want to win this contest.

I draw a model body. Then I put a pair of skinny jeans on the model.

Mary Ann looks over at my drawing. "Those look good," she says. She draws a long skirt on her model.

I don't love long skirts, but maybe Mary Ann will draw something cute on top.

"Your turn," she says.

I look at the jeans I drew. I draw a tunic top with flowing sleeves. I add little bits of lace around the neck and wrists.

"Nice!" says Mary Ann. She draws a vest with fringe to go above the skirt.

"Like it?" she asks.

I purse my lips and rub my head. "I'm not sure I do."

I'm trying to decide what it is that I don't like about it, but Mary Ann waves her hand at me. She doesn't seem to care if I like it or not. "Keep drawing," says Mary Ann. I can tell all she wants to do is finish the designs.

I add an armful of bracelets and a beaded necklace to my drawing.

Mary Ann adds a studded belt to hers.

I add some boots.

Mary Ann adds ballet flats.

I look at my drawing. I'm really happy with it. I hold it up so Mary Ann can get a good look. "What do you think?" I ask. I wait for Mary Ann to smile and say she loves it.

But Mary Ann frowns. "I don't know," she says. "Something is missing."

I study the model I drew. Part of me
thinks Mary Ann doesn't like my drawing
because I said I didn't like hers. But another
part of me agrees with her. Something is
definitely missing.

Suddenly I have a great idea. I add a big
cowboy hat, oversized sunglasses, and long
hair with bangs.

"Does hair count as part of the outfit?"
Mary Ann asks.

"It's a wig!" I explain.

Mary Ann frowns again. "I don't know.
I'm not sure I like the hat and the glasses.
Do you really think you need all that?"

I study my design for a long time.

"I *really* think I need it," I say to Mary
Ann. I'm not sure why, but I just have a
feeling I do.

"OK," Mary Ann finally says like she's
still not 100% sure she agrees with me, but

she'll go along with it anyway.

I smile at her. "I guess I'm done!"

"Me too!" says Mary Ann.

I study her design. It's good, but it could use a little something extra. "Do you think *you* need to add something else?" I ask.

outfit by
Mallory McDonald
← cowboy hat
Sunglasses →
← wig with long straight hair
chunky necklace →
Long flowy sleeves ←
Bracelets →
Tunic top with lace edges
← Skinny jeans
← boots

Mary Ann shakes her head like her design is fine the way it is. She takes a coffee mug of colored pencils off of my desk and hands it to me. "Time to start coloring."

When we're done, we write our names and addresses on top of our designs and slip them carefully into envelopes. Then we add stamps and lick them shut.

We carefully copy Fran's address on the outside of our envelopes.

I take a deep breath. I'm tired, but I'm excited too. "I guess we're finished," I say.

Mary Ann shakes her head. "Not yet. We still have one more thing to do."

She pulls me by my arm as she walks outside. She stops in front of my mailbox.

"Put it in," says Mary Ann.

I take a deep breath. "Do you think there's any chance one of us will win?" I'm sure a lot of people are entering this contest.

Mary Ann looks at me like a teacher looking down at a student over the rim of her glasses, even though she isn't wearing any. "I think we have as good a chance as anybody."

She takes the envelope out of my hand and lays both envelopes carefully in the mailbox. "We'll never know if we don't send them in," says Mary Ann. Then she crosses her fingers for luck. "Off they go," she says with a smile.

I cross my fingers too. "Off they go," I say back.

Then I plop down on the ground. Now all we have to do is wait and see what happens.

THE ENVELOPE, PLEASE

Fact #1: For the past four weeks, Mary Ann and I have been spending a lot of time by our mailboxes.

Fact #2: My brother, Max, says all the time we've been spending by our mailboxes has been wasted time. He says there's no way either one of us is going to win any contest.

Fact #3: George, the mail carrier,

arrives in approximately ten minutes.

"Hopefully today will be our lucky day," says Mary Ann. She plops down on the ground under my mailbox.

I plop down beside her. We've been waiting so long to get a letter from Fashion Fran saying one of us won the Design Your Dream Outfit contest. At first, I was worried about what would happen if one of us won. Now, I just hope one of us does. I'm sure we could figure out a way to both go on the show. I really want today to be our lucky day, but maybe my brother is right. Maybe we aren't going to win anything.

Mary Ann grabs my arm and points down the street. "Here comes George!"

He stops his truck in front of our house. "Good afternoon, girls." George smiles at us and pulls out a stack of mail. He hands it to me. He hands the next pile to Mary Ann.

When Mary Ann and I first started waiting, we told George what we were waiting for. For the first few weeks, he stayed while we  looked through the mail to see if we got anything from Fashion Fran.

I guess George got sick of waiting, because he doesn't stay anymore.

After George drives off, Mary Ann and I start looking through our piles of envelopes.

Boring . . . lots of ads and bills. Mary Ann leans over my shoulder. "Nothing in mine. Did you get anything?" she asks.

I shake my head from side to side.

"Just plain envelopes." I keep flipping through the stack. When I flip to a shiny gold envelope, I stop. There's something different about this envelope.

Mary Ann leans in like she senses there is something different too.

I drop the rest of the mail I'm holding and turn the envelope over. Mary Ann and I both see a New York City return address.

"It's addressed to Miss Mallory McDonald." My voice is barely a whisper.

"Mallory, open it!" I can tell Mary Ann is trying to stay calm, but her voice sounds shaky.

I carefully pull back the flap on the envelope. Mary Ann and I both hold our breath as I pull out a thick sheet of gold paper. I'm almost too scared to look. Mary Ann grabs my arm. Slowly, I unfold the paper and start reading.

Fashion Fran

Dear Miss Mallory McDonald,

Congratulations!

You are the official winner of the Fashion Fran Design Your Dream Outfit contest. You have been selected from thousands of applicants to visit the set of my show in New York City! Our seamstresses will create your dream outfit, and you will have the opportunity to model it on a very special episode of Fashion Fran.

It is my pleasure to invite you and three others of your choosing to come to New York for three days.

You will all fly in comfort and stay at a luxury hotel in New York City as my guests. Enjoy seeing the famous sights of the city that never sleeps! My staff will ensure that your trip to New York and your time on camera is an experience you will always remember.

Enclosed is another letter for your parents with travel details and the name and number of my assistant who will help with the arrangements. Congratulations again! I love your dreamy design!

I can't wait to meet you!
Fashionably,
Fran

"You won!" Mary Ann grabs me. She starts screaming and jumping. "You won! You won! You won!"

I would scream and jump too, but I'm too shocked to scream or jump. I can't believe I won.

When Mary Ann stops screaming, I unfold the letter to my parents. I start reading it out loud. Lots of stuff about hotels, plane tickets, addresses, and dates.

"Forget that!" says Mary Ann. "You won and *we* get to be on the *Fashion Fran* show!"

Mary Ann is my lifelong best friend.

We do everything together.

We paint our toenails the same color.

We chew the same kind of gum.

We like the same TV show.

We wear matching pajamas.

We say things three times.

We've gone together on vacations and to summer camp.

And we have a pile of scrapbooks that we made together.

I have always done everything with Mary Ann. We have lived next door to each other almost all of our lives. The first pinky swear we ever made was when we swore to always be lifelong best friends. I love Mary Ann with all my heart, but sometimes she says things that scare me.

And this is one of those times.

She taps me on the shoulder like she is talking and wants my full attention.

"You won the contest, and we get to be on the *Fashion Fran* show!" This time when she says "we," she holds up her pinky like she wants to make sure I remember the pinky swear we made:

"If one of us wins, we'll figure out the rest."

"I don't see how we're going to pull this off," I say to Mary Ann. My voice is almost a whisper.

Mary Ann crosses her arms across her chest and shakes her head like she's disappointed she even has to explain this to me.

"Mallory, when we were five, we made a pinky swear that we would share all our Halloween candy.

"Even though I got two pumpkins full of candy and you only got one, I shared all my candy with you.

"I kept my pinky swear!"

Mary Ann keeps talking. "When we were seven and you were scared to go to school, we made a pinky swear that we would sit next to each other in class no matter what.

"I was the one who had to convince mean, scary Mrs. Barton to put our desks next to each other.

"I kept my pinky swear!"

Mary Ann keeps talking like she's nowhere near done. "And when we were nine, we made a pinky swear to always paint our toenails the same color.

"There have been times when I didn't like the color you picked. But I painted my toenails the same color as yours. I KEPT MY PINKY SWEAR!"

Mary Ann gives me a what-kind-of-best-friend-would-you-be-if-you-didn't-keep-your-pinky-swear look.

"A pinky swear is a pinky swear," she says.

I take a deep breath. I know a pinky swear is a pinky swear.

I just don't know how I'm going to keep this one.

OPERATION: MOMS

Mary Ann sits on a bench while I pace back and forth in front of the wish pond at the end of our street. Mary Ann reads from a clipboard.

"List?"

"Check," I say.

"Letters and pictures?"

"Check. Check."

"Folding Chairs? TV table? Back pillows?"

"Check. Check. Check."

"Cupcakes? Lemonade? Fruit Platter? Mints?"

"Check. Check. Check. And . . . check," I say.

Mary Ann takes a deep breath. "OK. We're ready to put *Operation: Moms* into action."

We both cross our fingers and our toes. Then we pick up rocks and toss them into the wish pond. Hopefully, our crossing and tossing will bring us good luck. Right now, we could really use some good luck.

Operation: Moms is going to be a tricky one. We have to convince our moms that the four people who should go to New York are Mom, me, Mary Ann, and her mom. My mom is going to say Max and Dad should go. Mary Ann's mom is going to say she's not sure it is a good idea since she is pregnant.

"I'll get the moms. You get the

blindfolds," says Mary Ann.

I nod. Then I take one last look at everything we set up. It looks good. But still, convincing our moms to take us both to New York won't be easy.

When I see Mary Ann walking down the street with our moms, I run to meet them. "No peeking!" I say as I blindfold our moms.

Mary Ann's mom pats her belly. "Careful!" she says.

"Don't worry," Mary Ann and I say at the same time. Since Colleen's baby is due this summer, *careful* is a word she uses a lot.

We guide our moms to the chairs we set up at the wish pond. We sit them down. Then we take off the blindfolds. "Wow!" both moms say as they look at the table of treats in front of them. Mary Ann and I adjust the pillows behind their backs to make sure they are extra comfy.

Mary Ann's mom smiles. "What did we do to deserve all this?" she asks.

"Eat first, talk later," I say. Mary Ann and I serve our moms cupcakes, fruit, and lemonade. When they're done eating, we offer them each a mint.

Then they look at us like it's time to start talking.

Mary Ann gives me a *you're-the-spokesperson-of-this-operation* look.

I clear my throat and start. The first part of what I have to say is easy. I remind our moms about the contest we entered. I show them the letters from Fashion Fran.

"Mallory, you won the contest? That's wonderful!" Colleen gushes.

"I'm so proud of you, Mallory!" My mom gives me a huge hug.

I wait while they read the letter. I keep waiting while they talk about how exciting it is to have won a contest. Then I pause. The next thing I have to say is not so easy to say.

"Mary Ann and I want to go to New York together, with the two of you."

Both moms look at each other like they are not sure about that.

Mom takes the letter addressed to my parents and starts reading. Colleen shifts around in her chair like she is uncomfortable. Before either of them have a chance to say anything, I keep talking.

I explain how Mary Ann and I entered this contest together. I tell them how we have never been on a mother-daughter trip with just the four of us. I remind them that once Mary Ann's mom has the baby, it would be a very long time before we could think about going on a mother-daughter trip together.

Both moms shake their heads like that is not something that is going to happen.

Then they both start firing off questions faster than kernels pop out of the popcorn machine at the movie theater.

Mom looks at me. "Mallory, have you thought about Dad and Max? Don't you think they will want to go to New York too?" She shakes her head like she can't believe I didn't think of these things.

Colleen looks at Mary Ann. "Have you forgotten that I'm having a baby? How could I possibly keep up with you girls in New York?" She shakes her head like just the idea of it is tiring.

Mary Ann and I had a feeling this was how they were going to respond. We look at each other, and then we both pull lists out of our back pockets.

We start reading together.

10 Reasons Why We, Mallory and Mary Ann, Think You Should Take Your Daughters On a Trip to New York City Together!

Reason #1: It will be educational. (Don't you want your daughters to be educated?)

Reason #2: It will be exciting. (Don't you like excitement?)

Reason #3: It will be good bonding time with your daughters. (Daughter bonding is good!)

Reason #4: It will be the last chance for you (Colleen) to go on a trip with your daughter (Mary Ann) before your baby is born.

Reason #5: It will be the last chance for you (Sherry) to go on a trip with your daughter (Mallory) before Colleen's baby is born.

Reason #6: If you go on this trip to New York, you will not have to make any beds. (Someone in the hotel will do that for you.)

Reason #7: If you go on this trip to New York, you will not have to make dinner. (Someone in the hotel will do that for you too.)

Reason #8: If you go on this trip to New York, you will not have to feed your pets. (The hotel in New York does not allow pets, so you will leave yours at home and someone else will have to feed them.)

Reason #9: This trip will be FUN for your daughters. (Don't you want your daughters to have fun?)

Reason #10: This trip will be FUN for you. (Don't you want to have fun?)

Even though we said there were only 10 reasons why we think you should take your daughters to New York, there is a very important eleventh reason.

VERY IMPORTANT REASON #11: It is a once-in-a-lifetime opportunity to have a mother-daughter sleepover party all in the same room, all in one of the most exciting cities in the world.

Our moms look at the list, and then they look at us like they're not sure what to say. Even though I'm the official spokesperson, Mary Ann starts talking.

"Please, please, please!" she says. "Please say yes that we can all go together to New York."

Mary Ann gives me a *make-your-sad-puppy-face* look.

I make the best sad-puppy face I've ever made.

Our moms start talking quietly to each other. Even though we're close by, it is hard to tell what they are saying. I hear buzz words like *plane* and *hotel* and *timing*. But it is

Who could resist this face?

impossible to tell by their facial expressions if they are going to say "yes" or "no" to what we asked.

Mary Ann and I aren't taking any chances.

We came prepared. While our moms keep talking, Mary Ann and I hold up pictures of places to visit in New York City. We hold up pictures of the Empire State Building, the Statue of Liberty, Central Park, and Times Square.

Our moms look at the pictures, and then they look back at each other. I try to send a message from my brain to their brains to say yes.

Our moms keep talking quietly for what feels like a very long time.

Finally, they nod at each other like they agree.

Mary Ann grabs my hand. I feel like we

are in court and the jury is about to read their verdict. I squeeze Mary Ann's hand.

I don't think I can wait another second. And I don't have to.

"Girls," says Mom. "Pack your bags. We're going to New York!"

NEW YORK, NEW YORK

"So . . . what should our brilliant plan be for getting both of us on TV?" Mary Ann whispers into my ear for what seems like the three-thousandth time since our plane took off this morning.

I don't blame Mary Ann for wanting to get that figured out. I'm nervous about it too. But it's not what I want to think about right now. We just landed in New

York. There are so many cool things to see and do. I shove the tourist brochure that Fran's assistant sent to me into Mary Ann's hand and point to a picture of a horse and carriage. "Do you think we should take a ride around Central Park?" I ask, ignoring the question Mary Ann asked me.

But Mary Ann ignores the brochure. Her suitcase bumps into my leg as we exit the plane, and she asks her question again.

I know I need to answer her question. But I don't have a good answer.

As we walk out of the airport, I repeat the schedule that Mom told me this morning. "We're going to check into the hotel. Eat lunch. Then we're going to go to Fran's studio."

Mary Ann smiles when I say that like a visit to Fran's studio is the answer to our problems. "I'm sure you can work things out when we get there," she says.

It feels like the bag of pretzels and can of soda I had on the airplane are stuck in my throat. It doesn't seem fair that I'm the one in charge of figuring this out, but I feel like I am. "I'll try," I tell Mary Ann. Even though designing a winning outfit and getting our moms to bring us both to New York was hard, now that we're here, I feel like the hard part is just beginning.

Mary Ann and I follow our moms to a yellow taxi that her mom says will take us to our hotel. She also says that we're going to be amazed when we get there because New York City has everything.

"Do they have a wish pond?" I ask.

Both of our moms laugh.

"I don't think they have that," says Mary Ann's mom.

That's too bad because that is the one

thing I could use right now. As we leave the airport behind, I close my eyes and pretend like I'm at the wish pond on my street. I make a wish.

I wish I will figure out a way to get Mary Ann on Fashion Fran *with me.*

I keep my eyes closed for an extra-long time. I really want my wish to come true. I know Mary Ann wants to be on the show. I do too. I want us to both be on the show. Together.

I open my eyes when I feel someone's hand on my shoulder. "Mallory, look out the window," says Mom. She points to row after row of tall buildings.

Mary Ann and I both lean forward to get a better view.

I tap our taxi driver on the shoulder. "Is that New York City?" I ask pointing out his windshield.

"That's the East River," he says. "And that's the city in front of us."

"Wow!" I say. "I've never seen so many skyscrapers!"

"Wow! Wow! Wow! Wow! Wow!" Mary Ann says. She told me she's going to say one *"Wow!"* for each skyscraper she sees. But she stops after sixteen *"Wows!"*

"There are so many skyscrapers, I'd spend the whole trip saying *wow*," she says.

Both our moms laugh and so does our taxi driver.

I take a deep breath. I'm starting to feel like this trip is going to be a lot of fun. The sights of New York City are so exciting, and I am glad they are making Mary Ann think about something else besides the show.

There's so much to see as we drive through the streets of New York. "I've never seen so many stores or buildings or cars," I say.

"Or people!" says Mary Ann.

She's right. "There are people everywhere you look!" I say. There are people walking on the sidewalks, coming out of buildings, riding bicycles, and crossing streets.

"You'll see people out and about twenty-four hours a day," says our taxi driver. "New York is known as the city that never sleeps."

I dig in my purse and pull out my camera. "We're going to have to take a lot of pictures," I say to Mary Ann. I roll down the window and start snapping shots from the taxi.

Mary Ann takes out her camera and starts taking pictures too. "Our New York City scrapbook is going to be our biggest one ever!"

Everything that is going on outside our taxi is so exciting. New York is completely different from Fern Falls. We take pictures until our taxi stops in front of our hotel.

"We're here!" says Mom.

Small Town vs. Big City

Mary Ann's mom pays the taxi driver. We all get out of the taxi and get our suitcases.

"I can't believe we're really in New York!" says Mary Ann. I can't either. We start jumping up and down on the sidewalk. We scream together, "We're here! We're here! We're here!" I'm feeling happier by the minute.

Lots of people pass us while we're jumping and screaming, but no one seems to be paying any attention to us. Except our moms.

"Come on, girls," says my mom.

We follow her into the hotel.

"This place is awesome!" says Mary Ann when we get inside.

She's right. It's more than awesome. I look up. The ceilings are higher than my house. The lobby is filled with fluffy couches, fancy rugs, and vases of flowers.

"Let's check in and take the bags to the room," says my mom. "We can all freshen up, and then we'll get some lunch and go to the studio,"

When she says "go to the studio," I look at Mary Ann. I know I should be thinking about what we're going to do when we get there. But I'm not. And I can tell Mary Ann isn't either. It's hard to think about anything except how exciting it is to be in New York.

I feel like a candy dish. The only difference is that I'm filled up with happiness, not mints or jelly beans.

Mary Ann and I walk around the lobby while our moms talk to a lady behind the desk. Then we follow them into an elevator and up to the twenty-fourth floor.

When we get inside our room, I can't

believe what I'm seeing. There are two
huge beds covered in fluffy pillows. There's
a big window with long, fancy curtains. And
behind another door is a marble bathroom
with an oversized bathtub. But the best
thing in our room is a big basket of fruit
and candy on the desk. The card with it
says: *To Miss Mallory
McDonald.* I open it
and start reading.

"Wow!" I say. I pop
a chocolate into my
mouth. I don't know
if it is because they're
from Fran or because
we're in New York
and candy tastes
extra good here, but
it is the best chocolate I've ever had.

Mary Ann eats a chocolate too. She goes

To Miss Mallory McDonald,
Welcome to New York!
See you on the set.
Fashionably,
Fran

to the window and looks outside. "Wow!" she says. "Mallory, you have to see this!"

I go to the window and look out. There is an incredible view of New York City outside our window. I can look into some buildings and see the tops of other ones. "Wow!" I say. "I've never slept so high up."

Our moms look at each other. "Wow!" they say at the same time. Mary Ann's mom and my mom start laughing. "You girls sound like parrots who only know one word," says Colleen.

We might sound like parrots, but I can't think of a better word to describe everything. New York is *WOW!*

I hop on the bed and start jumping. "Wow! Wow! Wow!"

Mary Ann hops on the bed and starts jumping with me. "Wow! Wow! Wow!" she repeats.

We hold hands while we jump.

We both fall down on the bed on top of the big fluffy pillows and start laughing.

Being in New York is so exciting. I was worried this morning, but now I feel just one thing, and I can tell my best friend feels the same thing: happy.

I feel happy.

Happy! Happy! Happy!

THE UNHAPPY LIST

As happy as I was in the hotel, I am just as unhappy now. And I am not the only one who is unhappy. Mary Ann is unhappy too. In fact, if there was a list called the Unhappy List, both of our names would be on it.

Here's why:

When we first got to Fran's studio, everything was perfect.

Everything was perfect until Ernesto took us to meet Fran's assistant, Holiday. We went with our moms to Holiday's office to discuss "show day details."

That was when everything went from perfect to NOT.

First, Holiday explained what would happen on the day of the show. She talked about where I would need to be and what I would need to do. My mom asked lots of questions. I shifted around in my chair and tried to listen while Holiday went over the details.

Wardrobe.

Fitting.

Stage.

Model.

Dream outfit.

I tried to focus while Holiday explained that I would have to be backstage early.

A nice man named Ernesto gave us all a tour of the set.

We got to go backstage.

We saw the sewing room.

We saw Fran's dressing room.

We got to walk through the photo gallery of Fran's most fashionable looks.

We even got to have chocolate-covered strawberries and fresh-squeezed orange juice in Fran's personal snack lounge.

Mom, Colleen, and Mary Ann would all have front row seats in the audience. I even heard her say something about giving them special backstage passes for after the show.

But as exciting as it all was, it was hard to focus on what Holiday was saying when I had something of my own to say. I crossed my toes that what I was about to say would work.

When Holiday stopped talking, I started.

I explained to Holiday how Mary Ann and I are lifelong best friends. I told her how we worked on our designs together and how we entered the contest together. I told her that we like to do everything together and that we would like to be on the *Fashion Fran* show. TOGETHER!

I thought I said it all very convincingly. Even Mary Ann gave me a look like I had done a good job.

So I smiled and waited for Holiday to say something like, "*I get it. I've got a lifelong best friend too. If we won a contest to be on TV, we'd want to do it together too. Not a problem. You girls will be adorable together on TV.*"

But that's not what Holiday said.

All she said was, "Sorry, girls. Mallory won the contest." As if it was something we should've already known.

Then she pushed her chair back from her desk. She took a deep breath and looked at her watch like what I was saying was not something she had time to deal with.

Portrait of a Grumpy Assistant

My mom and Colleen looked at each other and shook their heads. They apologized to Holiday and said something about how they hadn't known I would ask such a thing.

At that point, I gave Mary Ann an *I-don't-know-what-else-to-do* look.

Mary Ann gave me a *make-your-sad-puppy-face* look.

I made it.

But it didn't work.

That's when I tried dabbing my eyes like the idea of Mary Ann not going on the show with me was enough to make me cry.

Even Mary Ann looked like she was going to cry.

But that didn't work either.

Holiday just shook her head. "Girls, only Mallory can go on the show. It wouldn't be fair to everyone else who entered the contest if we bent the rules. I'm sorry, but modeling on *Fashion Fran* is not something the two of you will be able to do together."

Then Holiday looked at her watch again and stood up. Our moms stood up too. I knew it meant the meeting was over.

But Mary Ann and I just slumped down in our chairs and looked at each other.

Like I said, both of our names belonged on the Unhappy List.

THE QUIET GAME

Ever since we left Fran's studio yesterday, Mary Ann and I have been doing two things.

Thing One: Seeing New York.

Thing Two: Playing the Quiet Game.

Actually, we have been doing a third thing, which is fighting. But I can't tell you about the third thing until I tell you about the first two.

It's not hard to figure out why we were doing the first thing, which was seeing New York.

The reason we were doing the second thing—playing the Quiet Game—was because Mary Ann was not speaking to me.

It started when we left Fran's studio. Mary Ann said we would have to think of a way she could be on the show with me.

I told Mary Ann I didn't think we could do that. I reminded her that I already asked Holiday if she could be on the show with me, and Holiday said no.

Even our moms said it was silly to keep talking about this.

But it was the only thing Mary Ann wanted to talk about.

So I explained again that I tried talking to Holiday. I told her I made my best sad puppy face. I reminded her that I even pretended to cry and that nothing I did worked.

I didn't know what else we could do.

Then Mary Ann got mad.

She said something about "trying harder" and not speaking to friends who don't keep their pinky swears. And that's when she stopped speaking to me. Since she stopped speaking to me, I had no choice but to stop speaking to her.

So, like I said, we played the Quiet Game. We played it the whole time we were seeing New York. Which, to be honest, did not make seeing New York as much fun as it should have been. We kept playing the Quiet Game until we started fighting.

Keep reading and you'll see what I mean.

THE STATUE OF LIBERTY

The first place we went was the Statue of Liberty. We took a ferry to get there.

Once we arrived, we took a tour of Liberty Island. We ate in the restaurant and shopped in the gift store. We bought Statue of Liberty snow globes for Max and Joey and Winnie. We bought postcards for ourselves. We took lots of pictures.

Sounds like fun, right? Not exactly.

While we were ferrying and touring and eating and shopping and photographing, we were also not saying a word to each other.

And that made our moms mad.

They said that while we were at the Statue of Liberty, we should not be thinking about a TV show. We should be thinking about things like freedom and liberty and justice for all.

I said (to our moms, not to Mary Ann) that we *were* thinking about those things. We just weren't talking about them.

Then Mary Ann said (to our moms and not directly to me, but I think she wanted me to hear what she was saying) that all people should have the liberty and freedom to go on TV with their best friend.

TIMES SQUARE

We also went to Times Square.

When we got there, Mary Ann and I looked at all the lights and signs, and believe me, there are a lot of lights and signs to look at. We watched a group of actors perform a song from a musical. We went into what I am sure is the largest Toys "R" Us on the planet, and we got to ride a real Ferris wheel and eat in a real ice-cream parlor inside the store.

Sounds great, right?

Not completely.

All of this looking and watching and riding and eating would have been great, except that while Mary Ann and I were doing all of this, we were not saying a word. At least, not to each other.

My mom said that all of this not talking was getting ridiculous.

Mary Ann's mom said that we were ruining the trip of a lifetime.

But even though they said these things, Mary Ann still would not talk to me, so I had no choice but to still not talk to her.

CENTRAL PARK

Another famous place we visited was Central Park. It is a very old, beautiful park. There are lots of trees and flowers and statues and fountains. There is a zoo, and there are horse-drawn carriages that will take you on a ride through the park.

I bet you are thinking that it would be really hard to do anything but have fun when we were surrounded by trees and

flowers and statues and fountains and a zoo, and taking a horse-drawn carriage ride (which is what we did) through the park.

But if that is what you thought, you thought wrong.

While we were doing all of that stuff at Central Park, Mary Ann and I were still not talking to each other.

I actually tried talking to her.

While we were on the horse-drawn carriage ride, I told her that I was sorry it did not work out that we could both go on the show. I told her that I really wanted us to both go on the show together. I told her I would NEVER break a pinky swear, but this is one that is not possible to keep.

When I said that, Mary Ann just looked the other way. I think it was her way of saying (or not saying) that she was very upset.

To be honest, I was starting to get just as upset as she was.

JOHNNY'S FAMOUS PIZZA

That's when the Quiet Game we were playing ended. And the fighting started.

When we left Central Park, we went to Johnny's Pizza for lunch.

Johnny's Pizza was filled with tables

covered with red-checkered tablecloths. The restaurant was packed with people eating pizza that looked and smelled delicious. Mary Ann and I got in line with our moms to order our pizza.

When it was our turn to order, I said, "Let's get mushroom."

Mary Ann said, "I want pepperoni."

"I said, "You love mushroom."

Mary Ann crossed her arms across her chest. "Not anymore," she said. "I can't stand mushrooms on my pizza." Then she made a face like just the idea of mushrooms on pizza was enough to make her sick.

And that's when I got mad. Really mad! Mary Ann has been eating mushrooms on pizza for as long as I can remember. It seemed to me that someone who had been eating mushrooms all of their life wouldn't suddenly stop liking mushrooms.

"I'm sorry that you don't get to go on the *Fashion Fran* show," I said in more of an outside voice than an inside voice.

People in line started to look at me, but I kept using my outside voice. "I tried to work it out!" I said to Mary Ann loudly. "But I couldn't. We are in New York, and you are ruining the trip by not talking to me!"

Then Mary Ann said, "I might not be talking to you, but you are yelling at me!"

That's when we started yelling at each other. I don't even remember what we were yelling. I just remember that our moms grabbed us by the arms and marched us out of Johnny's Pizza.

They said lots of stuff about how we were in New York and there are a lot of enjoyable sights to see, but a sight they did not want to see was the sight of the two of us not getting along. Then we all got into a taxi and went back to our hotel.

Mary Ann and I didn't get to eat the pizza that looked and smelled delicious. And to make matters worse, our moms made us say "I'm sorry" to each other for fighting. Then they said that until we could speak nicely to each other, we should go back to not speaking at all.

Unfortunately, the Quiet Game is not a fun game. Especially on an empty stomach.

THE GIRL WHO HAD IT ALL, ALMOST

A True Tale By Mallory McDonald

Once upon a time there was a girl who had it all, almost.

She was cute. At least, that's what people told her.

CUTE!

She was smart. Well, pretty smart, according to her teacher and her report card.

She was funny and had a sweet nature and a good sense of style. (No one actually said these things, but in her heart, she believed they were true.)

She had a mom and a dad and a brother and a cat and a dog.

She had her own room and her own bathroom (sort of). She had to share the bathroom with her brother, but she always tried her hardest to pretend she didn't so it was almost like she had her own.

She had a lot of joke books and a lot of colors of nail polish.

She was a good cook (at least when it came to making peanut butter and marshmallow sandwiches and chocolate chip cookies).

She lived on a street with her very own wish pond, and she lived next door to her very best friend.

To top things off, the girl won a fashion design contest and got to go on a trip to New York and appear on her favorite TV show. She got to bring her mom and her best friend's mom and her best friend with her.

You are probably reading this and thinking: "Wow! This girl has it all! I don't get the ALMOST part. What in the world doesn't she have?"

Well, since I am the girl writing the story and the story is about me, I will answer that question.

What the girl didn't have was a happy best friend.

And this made the girl unhappy too.

The reason the girl's best friend wasn't happy was because she was not going to get to be on the TV show with the girl. Since they have always been best friends, they have always tried to do everything together. They tried to go on the TV show together, but it didn't work out the way it was supposed to.

The girl tried to make it work out.

She tried really hard to make it work out. Really, really, really hard.

But nothing she did worked. And to make matters worse, she had promised her best friend that they would make it work out. She had even pinky-sworn that they would make it work out. The girl was the type of girl who always tried to keep her pinky swears, but she was having a

Portrait of a girl who always keeps her pinky swears.

hard time keeping this one.

And it was making the trip to New York, which was supposed to be amazing, not so amazing at all.

The girl's best friend was very upset with her.

In fact, she had hardly spoken to the girl the whole trip, and this very afternoon, they had had a big fight at a pizza restaurant. Even though she and

the girl made up after their fight (mostly because their moms made them), she hasn't said much to the girl all day.

Now it's the end of the day.

The girls are in bed at their beautiful, luxurious hotel in New York City. They are propped up against fluffy pillows. The girl is writing this story in her journal. The girl's best friend is pretending to read a fashion magazine.

The reason the girl knows her best friend is pretending to read the magazine is because there are big tears in her eyes and everyone knows it is impossible to read fashion magazines when your eyes are filled with tears.

This is making the girl very sad.

She knows her best friend is crying because tomorrow, the girl is going to be on national TV, on their favorite show,

modeling the winning outfit she designed. While she is doing that, her best friend will be sitting in the studio audience.

She would like her best friend to be going on national TV with her, but that is not going to happen.

She would also like to be talking to her best friend about how excited she is to be going on national TV tomorrow. But that is not going to happen either.

So that is why the girl has it all...almost.

AN IDEA

Last night, there was something I, Mallory McDonald, didn't get, and that thing was sleep.

When Mary Ann closed her eyes, I could not close mine. All I could think about was how upset Mary Ann was. I really wanted to figure out a way for her to go on *Fashion Fran* with me. But I could not think of a way.

I laid in bed for a long time trying to think of a way. I even pretended that I was at the wish pond and remade the wish that I made when we were in the taxi on the way into the city.

I wish I could figure out a way to get Mary Ann on the Fashion Fran *show.*

Then I tried to close my eyes and go to sleep, but it felt like my brain would not let me.

This morning, I woke up just as the sun was coming up. I don't know when it happened. But sometime between last night and this morning, I came up with an idea.

I think it might be a great idea.

At least, I hope it is. It is the only idea I could think of.

I shake Mary Ann's shoulder. "Wake up," I whisper.

As soon as Mary Ann finishes rubbing her eyes, I start talking. Actually, I start whispering. Even though our moms look like they are still sleeping, I don't want to take any chances. I don't want Mom and Colleen to hear what I have to say.

I whisper my idea into Mary Ann's ear.

It's really more of a plan than an idea. It takes me a while to whisper my plan into Mary Ann's ear because it is a plan with a lot of parts. It is also a plan that will fail if every part doesn't go according to plan.

When I'm done whispering, Mary Ann looks at me like I just invented a way to make spinach taste good. "You're a genius!" she whispers.

I don't think I'm a genius, but hopefully my plan will work. I don't know what else will.

Mary Ann gives me a serious look. "You would really do that for me?"

I nod. "We're best friends," I whisper. "And we made a pinky swear."

Mary Ann grins. "You're not my best friend. You're my best, best, best friend." Then she stops grinning. "Do you really think we can pull this off?" she asks quietly.

The truth is . . . I don't know if my plan will work. But I don't know what else will either. "If anyone can make it work, we

can," I say to Mary Ann. "But it won't be easy."

We cross our fingers on both of our hands.

Right when we do, the alarm goes off in our room. Mom yawns. "Rise and shine," she says. "We need to get to the studio early."

Colleen looks at the clock. "This is so exciting! Mallory, in a few hours you will be on national television."

"Right," I say to Colleen. Then I wink the tiniest wink at Mary Ann.

Hopefully, in a few hours, Mary Ann and I will both be on national television.

SHOWTIME

"Let's get a move on!" says Holiday when we arrive at the studio.

She takes my arm. "You're coming backstage with me." She motions to Mary Ann and our moms. "Ernesto will show the three of you to your seats in the audience." She hands Mom the backstage passes for the three of them after the show.

Holiday starts to lead me backstage, but

I stop. It's time to put my plan into action.

I cross my toes. "Um, Holiday, I'm a little nervous," I say. I try to look nervous, which isn't too hard because I actually *am* nervous.

Holiday rolls her eyes. "We're on a schedule." She tries again to get me to walk with her, but I don't budge.

I put my hand on my stomach

My nervous face

and bend over a little. I make a face like I'm really, really nervous and my nerves might make me sick. "I'd feel a whole lot better if my best friend could stay backstage with me."

Mary Ann rubs my arm and then looks at Holiday. "Trust me, you don't want to see what happens when she gets nervous."

Mary Ann gives a little demonstration of what might happen.

Our moms look like they are about to say something like, *"Girls, you need to do what Holiday says."*

Avoid at all costs!

But before they can say anything, Holiday grabs Mary Ann's arm too. "C'mon, we don't have time for this." She leads us both backstage.

Mary Ann and I silently high-five each other. So far, so good.

As we walk, Holiday looks at Mary Ann

and me. "You two look like twins."

We give each other a teensy, tiny *what-we're-doing-seems-to-be-working* wink. Part of our plan was to look the same. Even our moms said this morning that it was hard to tell us apart.

We both have on jeans and black, long-sleeved T-shirts. We both have our hair tucked into baseball caps. We're both wearing dark sunglasses.

We silently high-five each other again. Our plan is going as planned.

When we get backstage, Holiday leads us to the wardrobe room. She motions for Mary Ann to sit in a chair. She puts me in front of a bunch of mirrors. "It's time to get you dressed for the show," she says.

Seamstresses swarm around me like bees. They dress me in the dream outfit that I designed.

Holiday tells me to stand still while they make adjustments. She says not to move while they put on my wig, hat, and sunglasses.

When they're done, I look in the mirror.

I can't believe how good my dream outfit looks. I also can't believe what a good idea it was to add the wig, hat, and sunglasses.

I look over my shoulder at Mary Ann. She gives me a thumbs-up.

Holiday grabs my arm. "Let's go," she says. "You're on in ten, and Fran wants to meet you."

I gulp. I can't wait to meet Fran, but it's going to have to wait a few minutes. The next step of my plan is very important. If it doesn't happen, nothing will work the way it is supposed to.

I take a deep breath, and then I raise my hand. "May I use the bathroom?" I ask Holiday.

Mary Ann raises her hand too. "May I use it too?"

Holiday shakes her head like she's had just about all she can take.

She points to a door. "It's over there. But make it quick."

Mary Ann and I walk toward the bathroom. As I do, I make a mental map of the area backstage. I whisper to Mary Ann for her to do the same thing.

It's important that we know where we're going.

Once we get inside the bathroom, I quickly go over things with Mary Ann. We don't have much time. She nods her head as I talk. "Got it," she says each time I pause.

"Got it."

"Got it."

"Got it."

Holiday knocks on the door. "The show starts in five. Fran is waiting."

Mary Ann squeezes my hand. "You're going to meet Fran!"

"So are you!" I link my arm through hers, and we walk out of the bathroom.

Holiday takes a deep breath and shakes her head. She leads us both back to the dressing room.

When we get there, someone is waiting for us, and that someone is Fran. I suck in my breath. She's even more fashionable in person than she is on TV.

"Hello, girls!" Fran smiles at us. She has the whitest teeth I've ever seen.

Neither Mary Ann nor I can speak. I can't even believe we are standing in the

same room with Fashion Fran. I'm sure
Mary Ann can't believe it either.

Fran laughs. "There's no place for
shyness in show biz," she says.

Holiday must have told Fran why Mary
Ann is backstage, but Fran doesn't seem
to mind. Fran winks at me. "Your outfit is
dreamy," she says with a big smile.

Before I even have a chance to say
"thank you," Holiday checks her watch. "Two

minutes and counting," she says.

Fran nods at me. "See you onstage."

The next thing I know, Holiday is going over the directions she gave me the other day in her office. It was hard to listen then, but now I am paying attention to every word she says. And so is Mary Ann.

"It's simple. Fran is going to introduce you. You walk out, smile, cross the stage, turn, pause, wave, and walk back. Then, we cut to a commercial. You will model your outfit one more time after the commercial. Got it?" Holiday asks.

I nod. I got it. I look at Mary Ann. She heard what Holiday said and nods at me like she got it too.

A red light starts blinking backstage.

"Showtime!" says Holiday.

What happens next is a blur.

Lights twinkle onstage. The familiar

music that plays at the beginning of each episode of *Fashion Fran* begins. The announcer who does the countdown starts to count.

The next thing I know, Fran is onstage.

She is talking.

She is laughing.

She is modeling an outfit.

Then I hear her telling the audience about the contest. I hear my name.

"GO!" Holiday mouths to me.

I can't tell if I'm excited or nervous or a mix of both.

I walk up the stairs onto the stage. When I do, I hear lots of clapping. I look out into the audience, but the lights are so bright, it is hard to see.

I do exactly what Holiday told me to do.

I walk across the stage and model the dream outfit I designed.

When I get to the far end, I turn and pause. I put my one hand on my hip and wave to the audience with my other hand.

There's lots of clapping.

I smile at the cameras and wave again. I might have been scared when I first walked onstage, but right now, I feel like modeling on my favorite TV show is the most exciting thing I've ever done. My tunic top, skinny jeans, jewelry, boots, glasses, hat, and wig feel very fashionable.

I keep smiling as I walk back across the stage.

When I get back to where I started, I walk down the steps. I hear Fran say we are cutting to a commercial break.

"Two minutes until we're back on air," Holiday says.

I look at Mary Ann and nod. I would love to tell my best friend how exciting it was to model on national television, but now is not the time for that.

Mary Ann and I have work to do, and not much time to do it.

I tap Holiday on the arm. "I have to go to the bathroom again," I tell her. I hold my stomach and make a face like this time, it's going to be a real problem if I don't.

Mary Ann loops her arm around me like it's her job to hold me up and if she weren't doing it, I'd be on the floor.

Holiday looks at her watch and shakes her head. "You better make it quick."

Mary Ann keeps her arm around me as we walk into the bathroom.

When we get inside, Mary Ann and I nod at each other.

It is time to put the most important part of our plan into action.

I put on Mary Ann's black shirt, jeans, baseball cap, and sunglasses.

Mary Ann puts on my skinny jeans, tunic top, vest, bracelets, necklace, boots, hat, glasses, and wig.

We change clothes faster than my brother can change the TV channel to a game he wants to watch.

I straighten Mary Ann's necklace.

She tucks some stray hair into my baseball cap.

"I can't tell who's who," she says

Holiday bangs on the door. "Mallory, you're on."

I push my glasses back on my nose. With the baseball cap and glasses, it really is hard to tell Mary Ann and me apart.

Mary Ann fluffs up her wig. "How do I look?" she asks.

I stand back and inspect her. She looks just like I did two minutes ago. I nod like I approve. "Showtime," I whisper.

Mary Ann and I squeeze our hands together for luck.

Then I open the door.

DOUBLE
TROUBLE

I cross my toes that Holiday won't notice anything different, but Holiday is not in a noticing mood.

She grabs Mary Ann's arm and marches her to the side of the stage faster than Princess Jasmine crosses the sky on her magic carpet.

The red light backstage starts blinking again.

I look at Mary Ann. She looks just like I looked in my dream outfit. I just hope she can model like me too.

I can tell she's excited and nervous, just like I was. She turns around and looks at me. I give her a *you-can-do-it* look.

I can see the lights on the stage twinkling.

Fran starts talking to the audience and the cameras. "Welcome back to our very special Design Your Dream Outfit episode."

I listen as Fran talks about how many people entered the contest and how many good designs she looked at before she chose this one. "I'm going to ask our winner, Miss Mallory McDonald, to walk the stage one more time and model her creation."

Music starts playing again. It's Mary Ann's cue to start walking.

Holiday pushes Mary Ann up the stairs.

I cross my toes and my fingers as tightly as I've ever crossed them before. I hope we can pull this off. "*GO!*" I say silently. And she does.

I watch from backstage as Mary Ann walks across the stage. When she gets to the far end, she turns and pauses, just like I did.

She puts one hand on her hip and waves to the audience, just like I did.

The audience claps. She smiles at the camera and waves again. Then she walks back across the stage. Just like I did.

When she gets back to where Fran is standing, Fran wraps an arm around her. "Let's give a big round of applause to Miss Mallory McDonald."

I listen while the audience claps and the music keeps playing.

We did it! I let out a deep breath.

I can't believe I was on the *Fashion Fran* show and so was Mary Ann. Our dream came true. All our wishing and planning and pinky swearing worked.

"Isn't her outfit dreamy?" I hear Fran ask the audience.

There's more clapping, and then Fran talks some more about fashion and design.

When she's done she waves good-bye to the audience and says what she says at the end of every episode.

"That's it for today. See you tomorrow with more of the latest, greatest finds in the world of fashion." She blows a kiss.

Somewhere I hear a man yell, "Cut!"

The next thing I know, Mary Ann is walking down the steps back toward me.

As happy as I am and as much as I want to jump for joy with her that we were both on the *Fashion Fran* show, now is definitely not the time for that. There's one more part of my plan that needs to happen. And it's an important part, too: we need to change back before anyone notices we changed in the first place.

I give Mary Ann a *follow-me* look.

I walk toward the bathroom and so does

she. When we get inside, I close the door and lock it.

Mary Ann's skin is sparkly from the heat of the lights. "Your plan went off without a hitch!" she whispers. "I don't know what made you add the wig, hat, and glasses to your dream outfit, but if you hadn't, this plan never would have worked."

I don't know what made me add them either, but I'm glad I did!

Mary Ann hugs me. "We did it!" she says just loudly enough for me to hear.

"We're still doing it," I say.

She nods like she gets exactly what I mean.

I peel off my clothes and Mary Ann peels off hers. We change clothes even faster than we changed the first time, and I didn't think that was possible.

When we finish changing, Mary Ann and

I inspect each other. "Everything is just like it was before we changed," she whispers.

I nod that I agree.

Mary Ann and I both take deep breaths.

I have a feeling when we open this door, Holiday will be right there on the other side, waiting to take us to our mothers.

But I'm surprised when I open the door, and so is Mary Ann. Holiday is not the one who is waiting for us.

It's Fran. She looks at us with her hands on her hips.

"Girls," says Fran, "you are in double trouble!"

FACING FRAN

Fran walks us to her dressing room. She closes the door. It's just the three of us.

Fran's face is blank. It's hard to tell what she's thinking. I give Mary Ann a worried look, and she gives me the same look back.

"Girls, that was some switchup," says Fran.

I try to swallow, but it feels like there is a wad of gum stuck in my throat. "Are you mad at us?" I ask Fran.

Sometimes, when you ask a question, waiting to hear the answer is even scarier than asking the question. This is one of those times. She makes a *hmmm* sound. Then she taps her foot.

I feel like her *hmmm* and her foot tap mean she wants an explanation, so I give her one. I explain how Mary Ann and I are best friends and how we do everything together. I explain how one of the things we wanted to do together was to be on her show.

I pause. Then I look at Mary Ann like I need her help.

She picks up where I left off.

She explains to Fran how her show is our favorite. "We have watched it every day together our whole lives," Mary Ann tells Fran.

She keeps talking. "It has always been

our dream to be on your show. Together."
She looks down at her feet and shrugs
like what she's about to say next might
not make sense, but she hopes Fran
understands. "When Mallory won the
contest, we made a pinky swear that
somehow, some way, we would figure out
how to both be on your show."

I look at Mary Ann. Then she looks at me
like she's not sure what else we can say.

"We didn't mean to break the rules," I
say.

Mary Ann and I look at each other again.
"We're really sorry," we say at the same
time.

Fran looks from me to Mary Ann. She
studies us for a moment like she's trying to
figure out a complicated problem.

It feels like forever before she says
anything.

Finally, she does. "Apology accepted," says Fran.

She puts one arm around me and the other one around Mary Ann. "In fashion, creativity is the name of the game. You two certainly found a creative solution to your problem, and the show went off without a hitch."

Fran smiles. "I'm sure the two of you will

make excellent fashion designers one day. Actresses too. That was an almost flawless performance."

I scratch my head. Something doesn't make sense to me. I can tell Mary Ann is confused too.

"If it was an almost flawless performance, how did you know we switched places?" I ask Fran.

Fran smiles. "You can fool some of the people some of the time. But never Fashion Fran."

She looks at me. "When you turned, you waved with your right hand. Always a good indication that someone is a righty."

Then she looks at Mary Ann. "When you waved, you did it with your left hand." She pauses. "Sure sign of a lefty," she says.

Mary Ann and I look at each other and shrug. We thought of almost everything, but we never thought of that.

"You caught us," says Mary Ann.

Fran looks pleased with herself, like she's a detective who just figured out a mystery. "Even though we're best friends and a lot alike, we have one big difference. I'm right-handed and Mary Ann is left-handed," I say to Fran.

Fran laughs. "Even best friends have their differences."

Fran is right. Mary Ann and I might have our differences, but I know one thing we both feel the same way about is being sorry that we tried to fool Fashion Fran. We apologize again.

Fran holds up her hand like we can stop apologizing. "I don't like being fooled," says Fran. "But I understand the situation, and I applaud you both for finding such a creative solution. In show business, the bottom line is a good show. You girls put on a very good show."

She gives us both a kiss on the cheek. "It will be our secret."

I look at Mary Ann and she looks at me. We both put our hands on our cheeks at the same time.

I know Mary Ann and I have another thing in common now. Neither one of us is ever going to wash our cheeks again.

Ever!

ON TOP OF
THE WORLD

"Good-bye girls!" Fran waves and blows a kiss as we leave the studio.

Mary Ann and I wave and blow kisses back.

My mom and Colleen smile at each other. They're happy now, but they weren't so happy right after the show.

When they came backstage, they were very upset that we switched places.

When we asked them how they knew, they just said mothers know everything.

I don't know if that is true, but I do know that Mary Ann and I had to have a very long talk with them about "deception." And that was even after Fran told them that she wasn't too upset with us, as the show went just fine. She says in show business, the only thing that matters is what the audience sees.

The good news is that we finished that talk. And we still have a few hours left in New York before we go back home.

Mary Ann and I walk behind our moms as we leave the studio.

"I still can't believe you figured out a way to get us both on *Fashion Fran!*" Mary Ann says to me.

She smiles and puts her arm around my shoulder. "Thanks again for what you did for me." Then she gets a serious look on her face. "I'm sorry we got in trouble with our moms, but it was like a dream coming true."

"No big deal," I say. "You would have done the same thing for me."

Mary Ann grins. "If we ever enter another contest, I will do exactly the same thing for you." She holds up her pinky. "Pinky swear."

But I shake my head. "No more pinky swears for a while," I say.

Mary Ann laughs and nods like she agrees.

Our moms stop walking and turn around. "We still have one more thing on the agenda before we head home," says my mom.

"The Empire State Building!" Mary Ann and I say at the same time.

I don't know how we could have forgotten! I point up in the sky. It's easy to see the Empire State Building from where we are. "Can we walk?"

Mom takes the city map out of her purse and studies it for a moment. "It's not too far. I don't see why not," she says.

As we walk, Mary Ann and I talk
and point to things in store windows.
Computers. Shoes. Clothes. Suitcases.
Even air conditioners. No wish ponds, but
anything else you might ever want is in
New York.

There are so many things to see. "I don't
think I could ever get bored of window
shopping here," I say to Mary Ann.

"You might get bored of waiting in line,"
she says.

She points to a long line of people
waiting outside the Empire State Building.
"Do you think they're all waiting to go to
the top?" asks Mary Ann.

"I'm afraid so," says Mary Ann's mom.

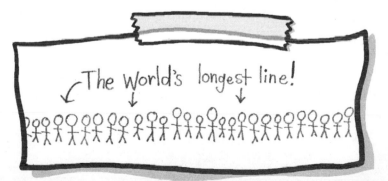

The World's longest line!

She opens her New York City guidebook and starts reading. "Between ten and twenty thousand people visit the Empire State Building every day."

We get in line behind a family with six kids who all have on matching red T-shirts and baseball caps. There are all kinds of families and groups of schoolkids. There are two old people holding hands. I wonder if they have been waiting their whole lives to visit this place. I look at the crowd. There are so many different kinds of people waiting to see the Empire State Building.

My teacher, Mr. Knight, taught us that the United States is often referred to as the Great Melting Pot because so many people from different places came to live in this country, and when they did, their cultures all blended together a little. He said another term for having lots of different kinds of people is cultural diversity. I think I've seen more cultural diversity in New York than anywhere else I've ever been.

"I don't think we'll get too bored in line," I say to Mary Ann. "Looking at all the people in New York is even more interesting than looking in the store windows."

Mary Ann nods like she agrees.

As we get closer to the front of the line, Mary Ann starts hopping up and down. "It's almost our turn," she squeals.

I'm just as excited as she is. We go through the security line and wait until, finally, it's our turn to get into the elevator. I can feel my ears pop as the elevator moves upward. It takes us to the eightieth floor.

When we get out, there's an exhibit on the history of the Empire State Building.

"It's like a museum in here," says Mary Ann.

It really is. There are Empire State Building facts and photos everywhere. Best of all, there's a gift shop. Mary Ann and I buy small models of the Empire State Building to take home to Max and Joey and Winnie.

"Ready to go to the observation deck?" Mom asks when we're done shopping.

"We're ready!" Mary Ann and I say at the same time.

We follow our moms on to another elevator that takes us to the eighty-sixth floor. When we get out, we are looking over what seems like the entire world.

"Wow! Wow! Wow!" screams Mary Ann. "This is cool!"

It really is. I don't even know where to look first. There's a tall glass wall that wraps around the whole deck. You can walk along each side of the deck and see New York from all four directions. There are people everywhere, but I don't care and neither does Mary Ann.

"You can walk around all four sides of the deck," says Mom.

We start walking and looking. We squeeze ourselves in between groups of people to get a look at all the different views of the city.

You can see everything from up here. Buildings, bridges, parks, rivers, cars, and people. Even other states! There are big binoculars so that you can look more closely at things that are far away.

"I can't believe what I'm seeing!" I say to Mary Ann.

"I know," says Mary Ann. "It's so different from Fern Falls."

I laugh. "I think the highest building in Fern Falls is five floors. I can't believe we're eighty-six stories up in the air."

Mary Ann wraps her arms around her chest. "It's windy up here."

"Very windy!" I say as I try to tuck a piece of hair behind my ear. It keeps blowing in my face.

"We should take pictures," says Mary Ann.

She gets out her camera and gives it to her mom. We pose in different spots as Colleen snaps photos of us on top of the Empire State Building.

When we're done taking pictures, Mary Ann stretches out her arms. "I feel like I'm on top of the world," she smiles into the wind.

I know exactly how she feels. Last year, Mrs. Daily taught us the expression *on top of the world.* She said it means a feeling of complete happiness. Right now, I feel like I'm on top of the world in more ways than one.

I met my favorite TV star. Mary Ann and I both got to be on her show. We're in New York City. And now, I'm standing on top of the Empire State Building.

I really do feel like I'm on top of the world.

I close my eyes and try to take a mental picture of all this that I can keep in my brain forever.

A few minutes later, Mom taps me on the shoulder. "Time to go," she says.

I think she can tell I'm disappointed that we are leaving today. She wraps an arm around my shoulder. "One more stop before we go to the airport," she says.

"Where are we going?" I ask. But Mom won't say.

"One last little treat for you and Mary Ann," Colleen says as our taxi stops in front of Johnny's Famous Pizza.

"No one was in the mood for pizza the last time we came here." She winks at us. "Hopefully, this time it will be better."

Mary Ann and I race into Johnny's. We order a pizza.

"Pepperoni," I say.

"Mushroom," says Mary Ann.

"Pepperoni AND mushroom," we both say together and laugh.

When our pizza comes, we both take a bite. It is crispy, hot, and delicious.

"This is the best pizza I've ever had," says Mary Ann with her mouth stuffed full.

I agree completely. Mary Ann and I both eat a second slice.

"Why do you think pizza in New York is so good?" asks Mary Ann.

I look out the window at the cars and the people and the bikers and all the activity on the busy street. Some people say the pizza in New York is so good because of the water they use to make the dough. Personally, I think pizza tastes so good in New York because you are eating it in New York.

And the truth is . . . everything is fun in New York. Even eating pizza.

I stand up and put my paper plate in the trash.

It's time to say good-bye to the city that never sleeps.

FRIENDS FOREVER

"Ladies and Gentlemen, please fasten your seat belts. We'll be taking off shortly."

Mary Ann and I buckle our seat belts and sit back in our seats.

I look across the aisle at my mom and Mary Ann's mom. They're sitting next to each other, smiling and laughing, like one of them just told a funny joke. They look happy.

I look out the window. I wish I felt as happy as they seem. But I don't. Even though our trip to New York ended up being great, I feel sad that we're leaving. New York is such an exciting city, and there are so many things we didn't get to do.

As the plane lifts off, I press my nose against the window and look at the sites of New York. All the buildings are starting to look like miniatures. I try to locate some of the places we went.

It's easy to spot the Empire State Building. Johnny's Pizza is impossible to find.

I look under the seat in front of me at the bag of souvenirs I bought. Max will like the Statue of Liberty snow globe and mini Empire State Building I got him, but I really wish I could have brought him back a pizza from Johnny's. He would have loved that.

As the plane moves higher, the sites of the city start to disappear below the clouds. Our trip to New York is quickly becoming a memory.

Mary Ann leans toward me. "It's hard to believe it's all over, and we're on our way back to Fern Falls," she says.

It's almost like Mary Ann can read my mind.

"It makes me a little sad." I tell Mary Ann how much I loved going to New York. "It was so exciting and so different from home," I say.

I wait for Mary Ann to say she's sad too and that there's no place like New York. But her answer surprises me.

"I loved New York too," says Mary Ann. "But honestly, I'm happy to be going home."

I think about what she just said. I remind Mary Ann about the hotel we stayed in, the sites we saw, the food we ate, the busy streets we walked on, meeting Fashion Fran, and being on national TV. "Everything we did was so exciting." I shrug my shoulders. "Won't you miss all those things?" I ask Mary Ann.

Mary Ann is quiet for a minute.

"I will miss all those things," she says slowly like she's putting a lot of thought into choosing her words. "But I'm going home with my favorite thing."

I think about the things she bought at the airport gift shop.

She's taking home an I LOVE NY back scratcher for Joey, a Big Apple poster for

Winnie, and toe socks for herself.

I give Mary Ann an *I'm-not-sure-what-your-favorite-thing-you're-taking-home-is* look.

Mary Ann leans her head back against the seat and laughs. "My favorite thing I'm taking home is my best friend."

When Mary Ann says that, the engine rumbles and the plane shakes from side to side. The captain makes an announcement about hitting some turbulence and making sure our seat belts are buckled. My stomach feels like it is falling out of my body.

Mary Ann puts her hand on my arm like she can sense that I don't like the shaky-plane feeling.

"Thanks again for keeping the pinky swear we made and figuring out a way to get us both on the *Fashion Fran* show.

You're the best friend a girl could ask for," she says. "As long as we're together. I'm happy wherever I am."

I thought I was happy walking the streets of New York and meeting Fashion Fran and being on national TV and standing on top of the Empire State Building, but none of that felt as good as what Mary Ann just said.

The plane levels out and I take a deep breath.

Mary Ann has been my best friend since the day I was born. We've done so many fun things together over the years. Going to New York was definitely one of the most fun, but Mary Ann is right. As long as we're together, it doesn't really matter what we're doing.

I look at Mary Ann. Then I hold up my pinky. "I know I said no more, but do you want to make another pinky swear?" I ask.

She nods.

"Best friends forever," I say.

Mary Ann hooks her pinky around mine. "And ever," she says.

We smile at each other and squeeze our pinkies tightly together.

We both know this is one pinky swear that won't be hard to keep.

A SUPERSIZED SCRAPBOOK

Mary Ann and I have made a lot of scrapbooks over the years, but the scrapbook we made from our trip to New York is our biggest one ever.

When Mom saw it, she said it's SUPERSIZED, just like New York City. And she's right. We just had so many good pictures to put in it! It was really hard to choose, but here are some of my favorites.

Mary Ann and I at the hotel

Mary Ann and I in front of the Manhattan skyline

Mary Ann and I with Fashion Fran

And Mary Ann and I on top of the Empire State Building

If you ask Mary Ann or me, we would both tell you that we loved New York City. But here's the funny thing about our trip: even though not every minute of it was perfect, when we look at our pictures, Mary Ann and I agree it was all good because we did it together.

Mom says things are always good when you're doing them with someone you care about.

I will say this: I don't always agree with my mother, but this time, I, Mallory McDonald, officially think she is right.

I'll say one more thing too. And since Mary Ann is standing right here beside me, we'll say it together: We officially loved, loved, loved our trip to New York City!

PIZZA, MALLORY AND MARY ANN STYLE

You already know how much Mary Ann and I loved the pizza in New York. But we like it even better on Wish Pond Road. Especially when it's cookie pizza. We found this recipe in a magazine. If you've never had Cookie Pizza, you have to pinky swear to us that you will try it immediately.

We promise you will love, love, love it!

COOKIE PIZZA
Ingredients:
One roll of refrigerated chocolate chip
   cookie dough
Small marshmallows
m&m's

Directions:

Step 1: Heat oven to 350 degrees.

Step 2: Press dough into a pizza pan.

Step 3: Sprinkle with marshmallows and m&m's. Press them into the dough.

Step 4: Bake for 10-15 minutes.

Step 5: Let your cookie pizza cool for 5 minutes.

Step 6: Cut into slices. Serve with milk and enjoy!

Trust us when we tell you that you will have as much fun making this as you will eating it. Happy eating!

Big, huge hugs and kisses!
Mallory and Mary Ann

P.S. This pizza tastes even better if you make it with a friend. We promise!

Darby Creek
A division of Lerner Publishing Group, Inc.
241 First Avenue North
Minneapolis, MN 55401 U.S.A.

For reading levels and more information, look up this title at www.lernerbooks.com.

The images in this book are used with the permission of: Cover background: © PhotoDisc Royalty Free by Getty Images.

Main body text set in LuMarcLL 14/20. Typeface provided by Linotype.

Library of Congress Cataloging-in-Publication Data

Friedman, Laurie B., 1964–
    Mallory and Mary Ann take New York / by Laurie Friedman ; illustrations by Jennifer Kalis.
       p. cm. — (Mallory ; #19)
    ISBN 978-0-7613-6074-2 (trade hard cover : alk. paper)
    ISBN 978-1-4677-0962-0 (eBook)
    [1. Fashion design—Fiction. 2. Contests—Fiction. 3. Promises—Fiction.
4. Best friends—Fiction. 5. Friendship—Fiction. 6. New York (N.Y.)—Fiction.]
I. Kalis, Jennifer, ill. II. Title.
PZ7.F89773Mad 2013
[Fic]—dc23   2012019008

Manufactured in the United States of America
2 — BP — 12/31/13

Clocking Out

CLOCKING OUT

The Machinery of Life in 1960s Italian Cinema

KAREN PINKUS

University of Minnesota Press
Minneapolis
London

Published by the University of Minnesota Press
111 Third Avenue South, Suite 290
Minneapolis, MN 55401-2520
http://www.upress.umn.edu

ISBN 978-1-5179-0854-6 (hc)
ISBN 978-1-5179-0855-3 (pb)

A Cataloging-in-Publication record for this book is available from the Library of Congress.

Printed in the United States of America on acid-free paper

The University of Minnesota is an equal-opportunity educator and employer.

UMP BmB 2020

For Richard Block, with love and laughter

Contents

Acknowledgments

For helping to stimulate this project, I thank the "Precarity and Postautonomia" group funded by the Netherlands Organization for Scientific Research; the Carolina Romance Studies Graduate Conference at University of North Carolina, Chapel Hill, 2013; graduate students in the Department of Italian at Berkeley in 2014, especially Avy Valladares; and Domietta Torlasco, Nasrin Qadar, and other colleagues who hosted me at Northwestern University. I am grateful to the archives and libraries that aided my research, including the Olivetti archive in Ivrea, especially Lucia Alberton, and Giacinto Andriani of the Biblioteca del Lavoro of the CISL (Confederazione Italiana Sindacati Lavoratori, Lombardy).

Of many friends who offered advice, help, and encouragement, I especially wish to acknowledge Michela Arleri, Diane Brown, Tim Campbell, Andrea Carosso, Luca Casali, Viridiana Casali, Ida Dominijanni, Mary Fessenden, John Foot, Luca Gibello, Andrea Ghirardato, Stephen Gundle, Cristina Iuli, Keala Jewell, Bob Kaufman, Federico Luisetti, Anna Maria Moiso, Renzo Ovan, Sabrina Ovan, Trevor Pinch, Gianluca Pulsoni, Paolo Rebaudengo, John David Rhodes, Kristin Ross, Maria Sepa, Joy Sleeman, Cameron Tonkinwise, Enzo Traverso, Lia Turtas, and the students who took my seminars at Cornell University, where we discussed many of the issues of the book, especially "Technology and Cinema" and "Labor and the Arts." Doug Armato's ideas and support for this book have been exceptional.

Opening Credits

A heavy curtain parts, revealing another curtain, which serves as the backdrop for the opening credits of the 1962 omnibus film *Boccaccio '70*.[1] The very same image reappears to introduce each of the four comic acts that will compose the whole (a *scherzo in 4 atti*). The curtain is distinctly theatrical and blantantly uncinematic. It bears at least two signifiers for the viewer: first, nineteenth-century stage productions, Goldoni, commedia dell'arte, perhaps opera; and second, the Italian television commercials, short sketches called caroselli, introduced nightly on the small screens of Italy beginning in 1957. These two interlinked references seem disjointed from the very first scene of the first episode we will see on screen: the floor of a modern Italian factory.

Films comprised of episodes by different directors were common in the 1950s, then faded out of fashion and returned with force in the 1960s. Mario Monicelli, director of the first episode of *Boccaccio '70*, titled *Renzo and Luciana*, did his share of them.[2] *Renzo and Luciana* was based in part on a short story by noted author Italo Calvino, who also collaborated on the screenplay with Monicelli, Giovanni Arpino, and Suso Cecchi D'Amico.[3] This film will serve as a jumping off point for a broader discussion of labor, automation, machines, and cinema in the early 1960s in Italy. To be clear, nothing in this film calls out for the microscopic attention I am granting it, but for that very reason—for its modesty and

A theatrical, uncinematic curtain inaugurates each episode of
Boccaccio '70.

ordinariness—it may have something to teach us. However,
before going into the film in depth . . .

A confession: I started out, years ago, with the idea of
writing a book about Olivetti, the office-machine company
known for its good design, graphically captivating advertising, innovative architecture, progressive social policies,
and experimental aesthetics. The family patriarch, Camillo
Olivetti, founded "the first Italian national typewriter factory" in 1908. The M-1, a machine for writing that bore his
name and the name of the Piedmont town where he lived
and built his factory, Ivrea, debuted at the Turin Exposition
of 1911, and from then on, the company was extraordinarily
successful in expanding its factory constructions, products,
and social programs.[4] Under Camillo's son, Adriano, Olivetti
shone in the 1950s and early 1960s with typewriters, calcu-

lators, telex machines, office furniture, brilliant advertising, and branding. Adriano patronized innovative architects for Olivetti headquarters and showrooms around the world. The company introduced both the first desktop or personal computer (the Programma 101) and the first transistor-based (digital) mainframe computer (the Elea 9003), developed under the patronage of Enrico Fermi, Italy's most famous scientist, and financed with funds left over from nuclear research. The brilliant Ettore Sottsass designed the housings for the Elea's modular units. Olivetti was one of a handful of Italian brands that spread "Italian quality" and "Italian design" to the globe in the period just before the explosion of the electronics industry in Asia.

Two parts characterize most computers, broadly: the con trols (human interface) and the arithmetic-logical components that the user does not normally see. In early computers, tubes helped to perform the "hidden" inner function. By the mid-1950s, transistors (solid state technology) had been introduced, signaling the advent of the digital in technical terms. Iron memory and magnetic disks programmed with specific languages allowed the machines to undertake batch sorting and respond to commands from a user to perform multiple operations in sequence. By the late '60s, integrated circuits led to what would eventually become semiconductors, which have now undergone generations of reduction in size and maximization of power. Olivetti's strength clearly lay in the area of the control pads and casings, the "human" side, if we like. By encouraging design and social research, the company produced machines that were both aesthetically pleasing and ergonomic and that, in a sense, seemed to correspond to and communicate with the user, sometimes even in a delightful manner: adult playthings, as Sottsass's designs were called.

With the sudden death of Adriano Olivetti in 1960 (and

that of visionary engineer Mario Tchou soon after), the company split off its "electronics" division (essentially computers, machines above a certain threshold of memory) and sold it to the American behemoth General Electric. The branch of the company that remained in Ivrea continued to make "mechanical" machines and a variety of products including office furniture, storage solutions, and so on. Over a few decades, weathering the transition to a globalized economy and competition from Asia in particular, Olivetti limped along with enormous debt until it was taken over by a financier, Carlo De Benedetti, who apparently cared little for the company's history or social goals. "Olivetti" joined a portfolio of other brands, goods, and services and fell victim (depending on your point of view) to globalization, automation, or greed, or some combination of these factors. It was delisted from the Italian stock exchange in the early part of our new millennium. A naturalized Swiss citizen, De Benedetti, along with other former managers of Olivetti, was recently acquitted after a series of lawsuits brought on behalf of workers who suffered the carcinogenic effects of asbestos, a material used widely in construction, to "protect" the space of the factory.[5]

Olivetti exists now only in the most skeletal remnants, but a rich archive of written and visual materials preserves elements of the company's practices. In researching, I progressively learned that there are already literally hundreds of histories of Olivetti out there, along with a number of novels by former employees and various short films, all with, to be sure, slightly different focal points.[6] Recent exhibits have highlighted the company for new generations in the post-typewriter age.[7] A made-for-television miniseries portraying the very concrete Adriano Olivetti as a visionary, was broadcast in 2013 by Italian state television.[8] The miniseries incorporates a subplot in which the U.S. Central Intelligence

Agency has Adriano under surveillance because of his social-
ist politics. Could spooks have been responsible for his death,
an apparent heart attack as he traveled by train to a meeting
across the border in Switzerland? Even the most hard core
conspiracy theorists in Italy have not considered this one!
More likely, as a former Olivettian told me, the Americans
might have been suspicious of Adriano's economic tendencies. But, for all that he leaned left and tried to cultivate a decent life for "his" workers, Olivetti was a for-profit company
competing in a global marketplace.

Some histories of the company are purely nostalgic, written by former Olivettians who pine for the two-hour lunch
breaks, during which they were encouraged to read books
from the company library while resting on verdant lawns,
and for the health clinics, cafeterias, sports facilities, nursery
schools, subsidized transport, housing, film screenings, in-
centives for further study, summer camps, and high salaries—
all provided by the "good father," Adriano.

With few exceptions, then, histories of Olivetti mark Adriano's death as a turning point after which the company either
lacked a coherent vision, was unable to compete with cheap
Asian technology, or failed to live up to his ideals about social
structures and territorial values (or all of the above). Other
accounts are critical, but only slightly.[9] Some studies were
published with financing from the foundation in Rome that
the family set up to honor Adriano. Some trace the history of
products and technology, while others describe in detail the
sociology and ergonomics of office and factory work. Some
place Olivetti in stark contrast with the harsh conditions at
the Fiat automobile company, headquartered about fifty kilometers away, in Turin.

Three Italian social theorists recently celebrated Olivetti
as "soft" and "smart" (both terms in English), and Adriano as

a figurehead for social justice and antifascism. As the head of a major Italian company, Adriano was unique, in their view, in his care for rural territories, a sort of "glocalism" before that term was in circulation. Adriano Olivetti represents an inspiration for contemporary movements of young Italians returning to the countryside and developing "sustainable communities" and "bioregions" (Bonomi, Magnaghi, and Revelli 2015). The company's legacy is not total degrowth, but ecological and artisan capitalism in comparison with the "hard" Fordism of Fiat, in this version.

A certain set of narratives emerge when one reads these histories or interviews of former Olivetti workers, or leafs through catalogues, or wanders around Ivrea today, or undertakes research in the company archives. At one point I even considered following the story of the site itself through the period of takeovers, when the main factory built by the Olivetti family on Via Jervis in Ivrea was used by the Interaction Design Institute, a school founded by Gillian Crampton Smith and dedicated to "design thinking," all the way to today, when it lies in ruins, only a part used by Italian Telecom (TIM, formerly Omnitel).[10] Tracing the narrative of Olivetti into the world of global finance with a whole series of different intrigues would have meant yet another book. And yet, even that book has been written, at least in part, as I discovered.[11] Perhaps I could have picked up the threads of technological history, moving from the glory days of the company through Arduino, an open-source, DIY electronics start-up that grew out of the Interaction Design Institute and still exists in the area. It could be interesting, I thought, to examine the success of this local-global company in the context of "maker culture" with Olivetti's history in mind. Some point to Arduino as an example of Italian know-how transferred to an enterprise that is more about a shared community of users

than it is about profits. Along with some efforts to promote
eco- or agro-tourism in the Canavese, as the area around Ivrea
is known, Arduino may seem like an alternative and uniquely
Italian response to neoliberalism. In the end, I didn't want to
write this history either. I began to feel there was little space
to intervene, and so, for a time, I put this entire "Olivetti project" in the drawer.

So, why mention this book not written? Because, as it
turns out, Olivetti still figures prominently in the following
pages focused on cinema and the early '60s. This moment is
crucial not only in the history of technology, but also because
it signals a simultaneous Italian dominance in the design and
manufacture of both "mechanical" and "electronic" machines
(to use Olivetti's distinction) and Italian dominance in cinematic creativity. In the broadest strokes, production shifts after the economic boom and new forms of social organization
solidify that will lead to neoliberalism and globalization, with
no turning back. But, if we want to freeze frames, the Olivetti
label opens up to possible trajectories and models of social or
industrial organization at a threshold moment when things
might have a gone another way. I will often call upon Olivetti
to serve as an example or counterexample as I draw on archival materials to help put forms of viewing or working into
some context, especially since, with some notable exceptions,
Olivetti was a company that spanned the blue-collar (workers
on the assembly lines) and white-collar (office workers who
used their products) worlds as they coevolved in a state of
interdependency for a brief period in the history of capitalism.

Ivrea, the home of Olivetti, lies about halfway between
Milan and Turin, the two most important cities in this study
and anchors of the "Italian industrial triangle," along with
Genoa, further to the south. Various key thinkers of labor
and machines studied Turin and Milan first-hand during the

period under consideration here. Raniero Panzieri, Mario Tronti, and Romano Alquati were among the philosophers engaged in public discussions, publishing important journals that would influence political practice and theory even up to the present. Some of the modes of production and industrial organization of the Italian boom developed earlier, notably in France and the United States. Italy copied forms of mechanization, automation, and organization from its more "advanced" allies. Precisely because the "rational madness" of Taylorism/Fordism arrived late and during a period of relative well being, it offered some possibilities for experimentation. If women working with the table system in a nineteenth-century French factory developed synchronous movements but were "not yet robots," then perhaps in boom Italy, there was still hope that they would not fall utterly into the abyss or become housewives whose unpaid labor, alongside increasingly mechanized devices, would help support new forms of male employment.[12] To evoke nostalgia for the stable social and personal structures of this era could sound reactionary, and that's bad. But it's also hard to deny a certain aesthetic pleasure that comes from a cinema that gently mocks superficiality and conformity with an attractive surface gleam, and especially because a film can make use of editing to focus on leisure while not denying the burden of the working day, pointing to minibreakdowns without the absolute "ego psychology" that corresponds to the American model of the "conflict-free," rational man who is well-adapted to his work schedule (Doray 1988, 114–15). Rather than bury the pleasure of the boom comedy or lash out at it in frustration, I ask the reader to take it under advisement.

Much ink has been spilled—or now, many keystrokes on machines that write both with ink on paper and on the displays of screens—tracing the development of automation and computers in the U.S. context. Take two examples: Jon Gertner's *The Idea Factory: Bell Labs and the Great Age of American Innovation* stresses the military origins of research on the East Coast, while John Markoff's *What the Dormouse Said: How the '60s Counterculture Shaped the Personal Computer Industry* hovers around the West Coast, with LSD and "alternative lifestyles" featuring prominently. Neither book mentions Olivetti, or really anything much outside of the United States, for that matter.[13] This is important to keep in mind. Italy was able to serve as an incubator for certain social ideas because it is off the international radar. Ivrea is practically invisible. Olivetti produced ideas and physical products that developed in an intricate relationship, while American companies generated unfathomable wealth for shareholders and venture capitalists by outsourced manufacturing. Olivetti played its part in a closed valley at the foot of the Alps known for a few early medieval castles.

One thing the present short book is *not* is an iconography of the worker in Italian cinema. Rather, it reads and weaves ideas and possibilities of work and life through a short film, *Renzo and Luciana,* one that no one would consider a masterpiece, a film so insignificant that it was very nearly not available to the viewing public. And for that, however, a film that is emblematic. Italian cinema history does offer a number of iconic scenes of *workers leaving the factory,* which is the title both of the first film by the Lumière Brothers and of a powerful reflection on labor and cinema by the critic and filmmaker Harun Farocki in 1995.[14] Farocki's documentary even takes us to 1960s Italy, with footage from Michelangelo Antonioni's *Red Desert* (1964). Strikers march on a street outside the walls of an industrial plant near Ferrara. They are not violent or even ebullient, but rather determined and robotic in their movements, almost as if striking were a quotidian activity.

Meanwhile, the scene in question is really an excuse for Antonioni to showcase Giuliana (played by the haunting Monica Vitti) in medium and close shots. She (and the camera) stand on the sidelines, exhibiting the utmost indifference for the plight of the workers. I have no doubt that Farocki's choice of this scene reflects on the duplicity: the sad parade looks and feels genuine (Antonioni as documentarian), while the shots of Giuliana that establish her impulsive behavior look and feel purely aesthetic (Antonioni as psychological auteur, a poet of neurosis). But, as intellectually challenging and visually stunning as *Red Desert* is, Farocki's choice of the strike sequence is perhaps a bit off. We don't actually see the workers cross the threshold from the space of work to the outside world. In fact, when Antonioni later takes his camera inside what is, for him, a beautiful space, we get access only to the factory's control center: a solid wall of knobs and meters surveyed by managers; the brain, but not the guts.

Farocki also leaves the space of heavy industrial production. For instance, he includes a scene from Pier Paolo Pasolini's first feature, *Accattone,* released just before *Boccaccio '70.* Women leave work at a Roman garbage dump, passing a pimp, the title character, who sizes them up. It's a grim picture of the possibilities of time spent "after work." The German might have been better served by Pasolini's *Love Meetings* (1963). In this documentary Pasolini takes his camera and microphone to interview workers outside a Milan factory. In 1968's *Theorema,* a journalist does the same after a shift at Innocenti (maker of scooters and cars). In both cases, the presence of the camera provides an opportunity for dialogue, and yet the workers are cautious in their responses. Pasolini's *Oedipus Rex* (1967) includes scenes of workers streaming out of Falck, a steel plant in Milan's Sesto San Giovanni neighborhood, known at the time as "Stalingrad."[15] Here the interplay between the workers' apparent lack of awareness of the camera/investigator and the film we are watching, most of which is set in a distant and orientalized past, results in a complex, perhaps even painful, dynamic.

A half century earlier, workers stream out after their shift in Walter Ruttmann's 1933 melodrama *Acciaio* (*Steel*). The director engaged actual workers as extras who realistically "perform" the gestures they normally do every day: clocking out, retrieving their bicycles, or striding toward home as they cross the threshold between work and life. He also takes us inside a plant and lingers there for surprisingly long takes on sweating, muscular male bodies and fiery hot rods that dance in front of the camera like animated abstractions.[16] At points, *Acciaio* looks and feels like Ruttmann's earlier *Berlin: Symphony of a Great City* (1927) in that its documentation of industrial strength dominates over a flimsy plot involving two rivals for a rather dull local girl. Indeed, Ruttmann was apparently the choice of none other than Benito Mussolini. Il Duce wanted a German director to showcase national power, while Luigi Pirandello, author of the novel on which *Acciaio* was based, lobbied for Soviet master Sergei Eisenstein. Pirandello would have preferred less focus on the machinery and more on the lives of the workers. In the end, *Acciaio* is above all a film that features bodies and machines inside a real steel plant (Terni, in Umbria), albeit not with the repetitious motions in real time that would be found on the Fordist assembly line. *That* kind of film (or better, that kind of scene) has limits, as Charlie Chaplin had established in *Modern Times*: the camera and the tramp go into the factory floor with the best of intentions, but neither can perform for long without the humanism of the actor intervening.

To be clear, other than a few seconds at the beginning, we do not see laboring bodies in *Renzo and Luciana,* which is now the focus of this book as it has evolved. Rather, the bodies that cooperate with machines to make the calculators, tires, scooters, cars, refrigerators, elevators, stoves, and small appliances we see on screen in *Renzo and Luciana* are like spectral figures behind the scenes. Film documents, but it also simultaneously withholds information, and this double game, played out in the interstices between what is offered for view and what remains hidden, offers inspiration.

On the other hand, the possibility of being together with and around machines in cinema is also intriguing. This is not because the films I discuss offer a humanist counter to the machinic, although that is certainly one possible response, and it is such a familiar trope that we may have simply discounted it into our own ways of thinking. The very masculine and violent response of the *Autonomisti* in the late '60s and early '70s—noisy, vibrant destruction of machines—offers another evolutionary path, one that would probably take us away from popular cinema and into more ephemeral or aleatory forms of filmic documentation. And, then, serious dramatic films that reflect back on the "years of lead" tend to fabricate a kind of nostalgia or narrative cohesion that defuses violence. Italy has its share of these too. In any case, contemporary with the making of *Renzo and Luciana* was the birth of the journal *Quaderni rossi* (*Red Notebooks*), an important incubator nurturing anticapitalist ideas that would develop in different directions later in the decade. Turin also saw massive strikes in 1962, at factories including Lancia (the workers won vacation days and better pay) and Michelin (the workers were unsuccessful, returning to the factory after several months of violent protests). Both companies had the support of Fiat, whose workforce in Turin was nearly one hundred thousand, many of them internal migrants from poorer regions of Italy.

Boom comedies appear, today, as smooth flows of (mostly) black and white images, tightly woven together to produce an effect of the real, even when the plots are themselves exaggerated. However, if we look hard enough, we may find cracks in the smooth facade of boom cinema where the machines (cinematic, productive, social, narrative) simply make no sense or break down. A particular scene may be inserted that should have ended up on the cutting room floor, by all rights. Or we are missing some crucial transition from one location or plot element to another. Sometimes, what we do *not* see on screen can be meaningful, even if we cannot rightfully attribute a fault in continuity or missing details or excisions to anything but chance or a random choice in editing. Stock characters or boom "monsters" (as in Dino Risi's comedy of this name), like the womanizer, the communist, the industrialist, the mother, or the whore, may fail to follow their parts to the letter. They may break the fourth wall in subtle or not so subtle ways. Tiny divergences between ideas offered up in treatments or early versions of a screenplay and what we see on screen may also be due to a series of logistical factors, rather than aesthetic decisions, but even these are worthy of contemplation. To be sure, the kind of neurotic close viewing implied in such remarks is not normally the way to experience a comedy (that is, a genre not necessarily intended for rewinding or deep close reading). It does, however, coincide with Siegfried Kracauer's notion that, since modernity is fragmented and nonlinear, an authentically cinematic cinema should also reflect this, and profoundly. Then, if we do locate hairline fractures in the smooth logics of (a) film, we might be justified to some degree in a metonymic leap, allowing that even the machines of industry are vulnerable. If machines on film, or the machine that is film, can break apart, then perhaps one might argue that legislative reform is not the proper response to the hardships of industrial labor. Instead, we might search for a language that posits itself as upholding meaning but falls apart or bursts into joy, or lapses in the logic of the factory. Its very intensity and brevity, the season of ramped up assembly-line production in Italy, make it worthy of study.

Fueling the boom, thousands of people migrated from poorer regions of Italy to Milan, Turin, and environs. Luchino Visconti's 1960 *Rocco and His Brothers* is considered by many the most powerful film to recount this movement. The Parondi family's arrival at the Milan train station, the city of lights and life as seen through their eyes through the windows of the tram as they take their first ride, and even the panoramic shots of the city from the roof of the *Duomo* are backgrounds for interactions between characters, but also simultaneously precious documents about the city at this particular moment.[17] *Rocco* ends at the gates of the Alfa Romeo factory in a vast industrial area on the outskirts of Milan. The viewer is not invited inside, but then, the heavy, repetitive work of producing cars would not fit easily with the rhythms and modes of this extraordinary piece of cinema. Ciro, the only brother who has found a job as an *operaio,* urges Luca, the youngest of the family to return to Lucania (an old name for the region of Basilicata, in the sole of the boot of Italy).[18] Ciro's final speech is, I think, highly ambivalent: on the one hand, "home" means the South and rural poverty; on the other hand, it also opens up the possibility that (a return to) working the land, even in subsistence-level farming, offers a legitimate alternative to the exploitation of the factory in the city. In an astounding book on Fiat, Marco Revelli interviews a worker from a town in Puglia, not far from Ciro's: "Life in Lucera wasn't bad. Under orders from our father, my older brother Severo was put in charge of the stove for dinner. He would send the children to gather dry wood and straw while he prepared for cooking. But for years people left, for Milan, Turin, Germany. They would come back for holidays. They had everything they could want and they talked about their lives as if they had finally found what they were searching for. So we applied to Fiat, and left. But Severo stayed behind. I recall I wrote to him about life in Torino and said it was possible to live there without being lost. He wrote back, talking of grapes and corn. And he asked me to send him some books on growing flowers" (Revelli 1989, 28; translation mine). Southerners like the one interviewed by Revelli lived in attics and basements, crowded rooming houses, and shacks. They may well have pined for the countryside, and if this is actually a very old trope in literature on labor, it takes on a particular nuance in the context of 1960s Italy, and especially keeping in mind Adriano Olivetti, with his compassionate colonializing view of the South. Soon after World War II, Adriano founded a political and social movement, *comunità*. "Community" for him meant a people tied to and shaped by the land (in the case of Ivrea, the Canavese). He worked toward constitutional representation that might replace the larger category of regions and the traditional political parties. He was even elected to Parliament under the banner of the *comunità* party. Clearly, his notion of "communal autonomy" had little to do with *Autonomia*'s anticapitalism as it began to form in the late 1960s and beyond. Rather, Adriano's writings are infused with a rhetoric of nature, harmony, and tranquility, a respect for agriculture against the accelerating needs of the cities. Interestingly, he found inspiration for his ideals in American small towns. Certainly, some of the notions of regionalism that Adriano developed still persist in contemporary Italian cultural production, and in the marketing of Italy for tourists, an important part of the nation's gross domestic product.

In contemporary Italy, nearly half of all residents of the

South risk falling below the poverty line, and economists warn of permanent underdevelopment of the region. There is little to bring southerners to the North, and today questions of internal migration are overshadowed by issues of refugees and migrants from elsewhere. Today Ivrea is a pleasant town that survives primarily on small businesses and call centers for Vodafone, Italy's largest cellular service provider.[19] A small number of shops bearing the Olivetti name continue to produce printers for specialty purposes.[20] The town government has attempted to attract tourists to their traditional orange-throwing *carnevale* (held in late February) or bring them in through initiatives such as a worldwide canoeing tournament on the Dora River. Predictably, there are several temporary employment agencies in town, and during the International Milan Expo of 2015, I noticed many postings in windows for short term gigs like hostess or guard. In what could only be called a bizarre twist of fate, the Convention of the Five Star Movement, the antiestablishment populist party that champions online voting, was held in Ivrea. One of the movement's principle champions and editor of its influential blog, Davide Casaleggio, born in 1976, made a speech, noting: "We are in the old Olivetti factory where the keys for the Valentine [type-writer] were made and where my father designed operating systems. Olivetti left an aura in this country and we wanted to channel this aura to begin thinking about the future" (translation mine). He made no mention of "old Olivetti" or of the company's history or its workers.

Some locals resist publicizing Ivrea and prefer to see it fade away. The Canavesi are by nature closed people, as I have been told on more than one occasion. While an "open air" museum guides visitors through some of the principal Olivetti sites in the town center, many of the factories lie in ruins. An architecturally ingenious subterranean apartment building built for Olivetti workers, the "molehill" (*talponia*), is now occupied, in part, by immigrants who work in the service industries in the area. Local residents warned me about drugs and prostitution circulating there. Slightly outside of the town center, a hotel once populated with visitors to Olivetti now houses refugees. The enormous Scarmagno complex, begun the same year that *Renzo and Luciana* came out, lies empty.[21] Some of Adriano Olivetti's holdings in the mountains have been cultivated for ecotourism, but the numbers of visitors are not significant. As I was completing this manuscript, Olivettian Ivrea was nominated by UNESCO as a World Heritage Site. It is not clear what this will mean for the town. It might serve to entomb the remains of what was a great experiment in labor and machines as a museum of the past, or it might encourage tourism and infuse cash for upkeep of buildings that will now, however, be off limits to future developers. Some *Epidoriesi* (residents of Ivrea) were less than thrilled to have their town declared a historical artifact, as they worried that no plans were in place to think productively about how to make the place viable for the future, whatever that might mean for a country with one of the lowest birth rates in the world.

In comparison, the former Pirelli Bicocca factory in Milan (where Monicelli filmed the factory scenes from *Renzo and Luciana*) has been dramatically reclaimed: one of the earliest factory structures is a giant hangar for contemporary art, including a permanent installation by Anselm Kiefer. Other parts of the "campus" have been transformed into research facilities and classrooms for the University of Milan. The brick Breda Tower, a symbol of industrial Milan seen in the background of Pasolini's *Love Meetings* and Antonioni's *La notte,* has been refurbished as a weather-research station and auditorium for public presentations. The Fiat Lingotto factory built after World War I in Turin, famous for its rooftop testing track and spiral ramp, has been repurposed by Renzo Piano into a mall and conference center. And so on.

For much of what has been discussed so far, Italy shares qualities in common with other Western economies in the postwar period. But Carlo Vercellone also notes a number of significant factors that are peculiar to Italy's industrialization: its relatively late development; the intensity and persistence of workers' movements beyond "May '68" (a decade or more in the Italian context) and even beyond the "years of lead"; the patterns of internal migration from South to North in the search for employment; the extraordinary poverty of the South; and organized crime (Vercellone 1996).[22] The strength of the family (in) business is another significant feature, especially if we place Olivetti and Fiat on center stage. In fact, Olivetti is interesting precisely because the company mass-produced objects in what some have called "democratized Taylorism": a kinder, gentler factory, for consumption by white-collar workers in offices, at a moment when innovations from the office also began to spill over into the domestic space. So, we can also trace the beginnings of a seepage or blurring of boundaries between work and home that may not be so pertinent for Fiat Mirafiori (based in nearby Turin, and at one time in the postwar period, the largest factory in the world), for instance. The paradigm of the factory spreads out: society is a factory, as Mario Tronti writes. The modes of labor and of resistance gestate in the factory and inflect (or infect) all aspects of culture.

Perhaps no other European country underwent the postwar boom with such creativity. This is not to deny that the *dolce vita* (Federico Fellini's film of that title dates from 1959, but the mood was simmering for several years before that) had its dark side, or was at best lopsided. But the boom was also a period when the republic was young enough to be able to move in different directions and Italians did not generally speak of the nuclear anxiety, social conformity, and militarization that characterized the period in the United States.

The boom was an interstitial moment to some degree. The immediate scars of the war were beginning to fade and the cinematic season of neorealism was past, even if its virtues, styles, and moods persisted. 1962 saw a remarkable series of Italian films on the domestic and international market, including *Il sorpasso* (Risi), *The Eclipse* (Antonioni), *Il mafioso* (Alberto Lattuada), *Mamma Roma* (Pasolini), *La commare secca* (Bertolucci's first film, released in English as *The Grim Reaper*), and *Salvatore Giuliano* (Francesco Rosi). The recurring character Totò (Antonio de Curtis) battled another recurring character, Maciste, a strongman who debuted in the 1913 silent epic *Cabiria*, in one of the many popular films in theaters. The Christian Democrats held power. The head of Italy's state-run hydrocarbon company (ENI: Ente Nazionale di Idrocarburi), Enrico Mattei, died in a plane crash under mysterious circumstances in October, the same month as the Cuban Missile Crisis. Were Mattei's plans to break the stranglehold of the "seven sisters," the big oil companies, simply too inconvenient? Was the American CIA involved? Conspiratorial minds are *still* sorting through the case. Two important works of fiction were published that year set in or around Olivetti: *Memoriale* by Paolo Volponi and *La linea gotica* by Ottiero Ottieri.[23] Olivetti sponsored *Programmare l'arte*, a traveling exhibit that begins in their flagship store in the Vittorio Emanuele II Gallery next to the Milan *Duomo*. Young artists, led by Bruno Munari, mixed cybernetic thought with design, and spectators at the exhibit would trigger a set of movements in sculptures and installations. Films taken at the time suggest that visitors were genuinely surprised and delighted by such kinetic interactivity (as they were during a reprisal of the exhibit held in Milan in 2013). To be sure, these Italian actors were not unique: similar experiments were taking place in France, Yugoslavia (the New Tendencies group), Germany, Brazil, and elsewhere.

"Cybernetics" and "feedback" were deployed in 1960s Italy without absolute precision. Italo Calvino's writings from the period address the cybernetic, as does Umberto Eco's influential critical analysis of modern aesthetics, *Open Work,* published in 1962. Poetry was similarly inflected. The Almanacco Letterario Bompiani of 1962, including work by Eco and other prominent writers, was dedicated to the question of translating the technology of electronic calculators to "moral philosophy" and literary production. Munari's cover for this literary yearbook is a graphic riff on a computer punch card, and the same artist did the cover for Frederick Pollock's *Automation: A Study of Its Economic and Social Consequences* in its Italian translation published by Einaudi in Turin, an outline of the back of a man surrounded by dots, perhaps meant to represent the punches on a memory card. Automatic writing by Nanni Balestrini played with questions of the autonomy of the work of art. For the most part, the movements and works associated with the cybernetic aesthetic remained removed from popular or working-class culture.

Although, as mentioned, workers did strike during the early '60s, this period predates the full-blown rise of a politics of *Autonomia* (autonomy from wages, from the constraints that capital imposes on definitions of life) and *Operaismo,* workerism, the imperative that workers themselves should seize the ability to remake such definitions. These two intertwined movements still exercise influence on political culture today both within and beyond Italy, both directly and indirectly.

From this point, one could follow trajectories of technology, design, literature, and especially cinema that pass through the postwar, through the boom and postboom, through the radical political struggles of the "the hot autumn" (of '69) and "years of lead" (the '70s), toward privatization and globalization, into post-Fordist production, and into the present age of the digital, the sharing or "gig" economy, the precariat, and a new rise of automation, and beyond. Traces of *Autonomist* thought persist in current proposals for a guaranteed basic minimum wage, and some of these proposals come from the right of the political spectrum—a strange twist of fate, as they replace other forms of entitlement and welfare. On the left, actors invoke postautonomist modes of resistance for activism around issues such as the environment.

However, if we wanted to write a history of machines that involves a history of radical politics, Olivetti would probably have to disappear. Olivetti, with its focus on what Adriano called "the dignity of work," is especially interesting precisely because it doesn't line up easily with models that *Autonomia* and *Operaismo* opposed. As Pier Vittorio Aureli notes, it serves as a negative example of how the movements tried to create something different from capitalism.

Olivetti was successful in expanding and innovative in its factory constructions and social programs, but above all, it made objects and environments for use in the world of white-collar work. The case of Ettore Sottsass is emblematic here. In 1954, the designer/artist had been affiliated with the Imaginist Bauhaus, a precursor to the Situationist International. But, after a few years, he either was booted or left on his own (Sadler 1998, 5). He apparently found his comrades too aggressive and unprofessional. Or maybe he lacked the revolutionary spirit they required from their members. Or a bit of both. Sottsass himself has been the subject of major international retrospectives that celebrate his colorful, playful designs, including work he did for Olivetti, such as the modular housings for the Elea computer and the youthful red plastic Valentine typewriter.[24] Sottsass, Munari, and others who produced "good design" for Olivetti exist on the other side of a divide: innovative, yes, but capitulating to a system.

According to the ethos of *Autonomia,* capitalism is not a rational system that can be made more rational through planning, and so, to engage in an appreciation of the aesthetics of such design work is also to think outside of traditionally defined leftist politics. Although the first-person introspection may seem intrusive, I have come to ask whether my attraction to the Olivetti designs is also, to some degree, a desire for the benign patriarch who would provide structure, meaning, and a narrative to the question of life and work. I wouldn't normally write about myself, but this is one of those moments when self-reflection kicks in, and it seems worthwhile putting this out there. What are the further implications of this kind of attraction, and can they really be addressed in a more neutral and depersonalized voice expected of traditional academic writing? And then, is it worthwhile to construct or seek out conceptual or historical bridges between *Autonomia,* the political movement, and "automation," a word that will appear often in this book? The former seems to want to destroy the latter, but this turns out to be a difficult knot to untangle, especially since, in the period in question, automation signals the promise of a kind of autonomy understood as "freedom" in a broadest sense. To be sure, "autonomy" appears in a wide variety of different contexts. Decades before the left political movement, a Fascist critic suggested "autonomy" as an antidote to naturalism, as a quality that might be applied in a positive sense to characters that exhibit "human qualities linked to the spirituality of the artist" (cited in Ben-Ghiat 1995, 640).

In the 1950s, *Autonomia* meant that Adriano Olivetti could develop his company on the model of a foundation, without pressures from the state or public ownership.[25] Aesthetic autonomy is a term that, for Italy, may signify work not bound to a particular political party. Or "autonomy" may be used to mean something like "rational" or "unbiased," applying the very language of Olivetti to the company's own social innovations: "the autonomy" of social services as a kind of "rational distancing" from the same services originally performed on a voluntary basis," or the "autonomous stability and development of social services" that are "democratically administered" as of the highest importance for the company. One might hear an echo of "autonomous" in the suggestion that existing trade unions must cease affiliation with political parties if they are to fulfill the function of worker advocacy. "Individual autonomy" is the goal of child rearing, something that the Olivetti preschool strives toward in its "replacement" of working mothers.[26] In fact, Olivetti turns out to be a significant laboratory in which such questions can be cultivated and studied. Today, "autonomous worker" is another name in Italy for a freelancer, temp, or "gigger." It's an ambiguous category that allows someone to declare income and potentially reap unemployment benefits but also lacks security and continuity. Similarly, "automation" and "machine" can refer to various things, including the cinematic apparatus itself. And this is to say nothing of related terms such as "robot," "automaton," "cybernetics," and "artificial intelligence," all of which are invoked today in discussions of both the present and future of work. Beyond terminology or morphology, what happens when cinema and machines (or cinema *as* machine) reveal gaps or cracks or break down or open up to uses other than those they were destined for, or when they disrupt familiar narratives? These narratives do have something to offer today, not only because they can be blown apart or reinforced, but also because we might find in them, especially in the machines of '60s Italy, apertures, contradictions, and possibilities that things might have gone otherwise.

Boccaccio '70 was conceived by Cesare Zavattini, the ideological father of Italian neorealism. Za, as he was known, never renounced the politico-socio engagement he developed around cinema in the immediate postwar period when he worked on treatments and screenplays for canonical neorealist films such as *Shoeshine, Bicycle Thieves, Umberto D.,* and others. He evolved. In this case, with support from producers, he gave some initial prompts to the directors, who also included Visconti, Fellini, and Vittorio De Sica.[27] They were supposed to create works of a "Boccaccian" nature: joyful, free, and "typically Italian"; festive, grotesque, pagan; and above all, contrasting the sexophobic prudishness that characterized bourgeois Italian society of the postwar period.[28] To varying degrees, the directors complied.

Renzo and Luciana turned out to be the least Boccaccian episode of the film. Monicelli was, at least according to his own statements in writing and in interviews, motivated primarily by a desire to portray the proletarian/petty-bourgeois world of Milan during the economic boom (roughly 1958–1963). While telling his tale, he turns a quasi-documentary, almost a neorealist, lens toward the city itself. Rather than bawdy or tricky, his style in *Renzo and Luciana* is closer to the genre known as the *commedia all'italiana,* the "boom comedy."[29] Films in this category include Monicelli's own *I soliti ignoti* (*Big Deal on Madonna Street;* 1958) and *La grande guerra* (*The Great War;* 1959) and any number of works directed by Risi, such as *Una vita difficile* (*A Difficult Life;* 1961), *Il sorpasso* (which, as noted, appeared the same year as *Renzo and Luciana*), or *I mostri* (*The Monsters;* 1963). Lattuada's *Il mafioso,* like *Renzo and Luciana,* even grants us a brief view into the workings of a Milanese factory (Innocenti). All of these films could be characterized as "naturalized, stylistically unmarked cinema" comprised of "transparent stories" (De Vincenti 2001,14).

In contrast to *Renzo and Luciana,* which revolves around a couple, most Italian boom comedies feature a male protagonist (actors associated with the genre included Alberto Sordi, Vittorio Gassman, Ugo Tognazzi, Marcello Mastroianni, and Totò) who is filled with bravura and energy but at times undone by the speed of social change and new wealth, a man who has difficulty playing the part of a modern Italian subject or "adhering to the grotesque social parade of normative ideological values" that mark the transition from the provincial *Italietta* of Fascism to a modern Republic (De Vincenti 2001,14). Maurizio Grande, an astute critic of the boom comedy, writes that the characters played by Sordi and Gassman exhibit an outward cynicism while they also retreat into the comforting familiarity of failure and "the forced adaptation to the real." In the dialectic between an excess of conformity and an excess of dissonance with regard to social values and conduct, the comic subject finds himself divided between his public image (what Grande calls the "mask of performance") and "the drives of an inapt and repressed subjectivity" (Grande 2003, 51; translation mine). The male in the boom comedy risks losing his sense of self. He holds no deep convictions, and while he fears being excluded from the masses of his compatriots, he is simply unable to conform, so he becomes a puppet, Grande argues. The boom comedy tends toward the melancholic, and it is not primarily slapstick. Italians might laugh at the foibles of workers who do not quite live up to the "American" modes that are introduced to them through an apparently one-way trajectory. In films like *L'impiegato* (*The Worker*) or Ugo Gregoretti's *Il pollo ruspante*

(*Free Range Chicken*), his gem of a short from the omnibus *RoGoPaG*, managers trained in America come to Italy, bringing the latest in office management, ergonomics, and public relations to a national viewership that seems in some sense to define itself as constitutionally oppositional. In any case, the bungling does not lead immediately to or even suggest any sort of consciousness, whether class or political, or even the sort of self-awareness with regard to sexuality, the family, and conformity that Pasolini wished for a couple of newlyweds at the end of his *Love Meetings*.

As in that film, though, female characters actually come off much better in the boom comedies, as they often appear both more concrete and much better adapted to the future than the males. But above all, whether they are workers, aspiring bourgeoisie, or the wives of the factory owners, the actresses are gorgeous objects to be enjoyed on screen. They cannot shed this quality, no matter what position they take up within the narrative structure of the comedy. This is what cinema does, whereas a laboring woman in a novel lacks this aspect—not exactly breaking news to anyone who has read introductory film theory. But, while it's not a startling revelation, it is still worth noting that we tend to forget or normalize the gendered division of labor in a genre or style of filmmaking that is primarily about men. In any case, for its cinematography, the director's commitments, the plot, the choices of locations, and so on, *Renzo and Luciana* fits within a fairly established set of conventions.

Italian national cinema has long been understood from inside and out as a cinema of the human, as (neo)realism, where all other forms or genres of cinema are secondary, minor, and less authentic. Implicitly, then, Italian cinema should be a cinema of the human body moving in synchronicity with the functions to which it is subject, and thus a cinema in which the automatic nature of the apparatus itself must be suppressed, repressed, hidden, or smashed. Perhaps no author has understood this more profoundly than did Pirandello in the early twentieth century. His novel *Quaderni di Serafino Gubbio operatore* (translated as *Shoot!*) is written as a series of notebooks or observations from the point of view of a camera operator named Serafino, who is not unlike the alien/robot in Gregoretti's 1960s sci-fi comedy *Omicron* who films/writes what he sees in order to send back information to the home planet to help them conquer the earth and put its inhabitants in servitude. Serafino does not "work" in a strict sense ("io non opero niente," he notes). Once the actors are in place on the set, a film director calls out to Serafino the number of meters of film required for a given shot. The operator cuts them and winds them in place. He then turns the camera mechanism until the director calls out to stop. Serafino's job, he recognizes, could easily be done by a machine or a monkey. Incidentally, this is the same remark we will hear from Lulù, a factory worker in Elio Petri's film *The Working Class Goes to Heaven*. The monkey becomes a cipher for a certain antiautomation discourse in writings against the social alienation produced by the factory. More significantly, though, for Serafino, his job *requires* his very passivity with regard to the action before him. Pirandello places in Serafino's words the idea that man has become a servant or even a slave of the machines he built. This all-too-humanist idea is partially significant, but also partially misses the point. Pirandello critiques the inhuman pace of life in the city and the industry of producing culture, where cinema is mechanized and theater not. He is writing about the existential significance of being a human in the age of the machines, but he is not writing about the factory. So how far can we take his model for this study?

Cesare Zavattini's manifesto, "Some Ideas on Cinema"

(1952), posited a woman buying a pair of shoes as the signature subject for an ideal film. If we must resort to fully developed or Hollywood-style stories, these are simply compromises with a medium that, in its most ideal form, should be pure representation. Likewise, Kracauer's brilliant manifesto on cinema as "redemption of physical reality" highlights the potential of the cinema not just to represent reality, but to become reality. Certainly, Pirandello, Zavattini, and Kracauer all wrote before Italian factory work was ramped up to the levels responded to by the *Autonomisti* beginning later in the 1960s. But that isn't really the point, because Italian cinema was (and perhaps still is, to the degree that it is a cinema of nostalgia about its cinematic heritage) focused on mapping the social and urban consequences of the broader economy without lingering on the work itself. Most of the protagonists of the great neorealist films are in between jobs, retired, or underemployed. They have not made it to the factory (yet). If they were to find employment on the assembly line, then familiar forms of neorealist-inspired cinema might have to adjust to capture their daily lives or reject them as subjects altogether.

1

The Clock in the Factory

The director's name and film's title are imposed over a large clock in a factory after the curtain opens on *Renzo and Luciana*.[1]

In the very first motion picture, the Lumières' *Workers Leaving the Factory*, a sound triggers the end of the workday. Or so we assume. We do not hear this sound, because the technology of the film has not yet incorporated it. Yet we witness a flow of bodies, all headed out of the frame. We ourselves supply that divide between the noise and signal because we know that is what happens in real life, but the image we perceive on screen is itself what lies at the origin of cinema.

The clock is a machine with a face, potentially like a robot, but it does not produce. Still, the analogical relations among the face, the mechanisms of the clock, and the human body are so deeply rooted in the factory that they cannot readily be separated into their component parts. By its nature, the clock represents a time that is understood to be out of joint with the times of the human body. The clock could be the emblem of collective life in the same way that the bell was the symbol of collective life in the village before the coming of the factory. "The factory is a watch, but human labor is also regulated as though it were a watch" (Doray 1988, 67). The clock is like the watch worn by the individuals of the collective, but synchronized to the factory, just as the chronometer's stopwatch respects the same units of time but now subdivides them into

When the second hand hits **12**, a siren sounds and workers scamper.

parcels that equate to the speed of production. But both are collective only in the sense of being antihuman or robotic.

This particular clock in *Renzo and Luciana*—apparently meant to measure movements in the factory, and not to tell the time of day—has only a second hand.[2] During the working day, it must go around and around, we imagine, to signal micromovements of production, but we viewers come on the scene at a very particular moment during that day. We don't have long to wait. When the hand hits 12, a siren sounds, marking the end of the morning shift. In this sense, this particular clock is quite idiosyncratic, and even disorienting, but the casual viewer of this film would have (literally) no time to register this, for we move immediately away, having experienced only the coincidence of "clock + siren." The workers (many of them women) spring up immediately. They have no libidinal or professional attachment to what they are doing, nothing to wrap up. They are programmed, just like machines that, in fact, continue to function even as the workers scamper away with Pavlovian reflexes.

Because the scene is so brief, the viewer also has no time to think about the time of the working day or productivity. But, on reflection, a clock is not what we might call cinematic. It floats there on the screen, its face staring blankly back at the audience. The artist Christian Marclay used two techniques for his 2010 work *The Clock,* if we can even call them that, to recall both the clock's dumb stasis and then, precisely because of this, how the on-screen clock functions as a significant clue to every mystery: editing and research or data mining (intercutting of clocks corresponding to every single minute of a twenty-four-hour cycle).[3] Because it cannot but register one particular time on screen, the clock serves as a kind of ontol ogy in or of cinema. The clock in the factory also plays this dumb-faced role. It may be mechanically (or later, digitally) linked to a bell or whistle. Workers may clock-watch, but if they do, time will pass more slowly than it would if they focused on the pieces in front of them or any other number of tasks on a spectrum from highly repetitive to highly social and interactive. The clock doesn't care: it is there to remind workers and viewers of the fact that, at some point, the workers will be allowed to leave the place and enter the outside world; they will, in fact, be required to leave, for occupation is insurrection.

In any case, this brief sequence of clock and heavy machinery as background to the opening credits is as close as we get in *Renzo and Luciana* to a view of everyday life in the factory. Why should we expect a film to teach about work? "Factories have not attracted film," a voice-over explains in Farocki's *Workers Leaving the Factory.* "Rather, they have repelled it." In general, it was difficult for directors of fictional films to gain access to the spaces of actual production in Italy, as in other European countries at the time. Monicelli's next film after *Renzo and Luciana* was *I compagni* (*The Organizer*), set in a "hot" nineteenth-century textile factory, a displacement of attention from the here and now of actual struggles.[4] Monicelli did some establishing work in Turin, but the bulk of *I compagni* was shot in the town of Cuneo nearby and in a factory in Zagreb, where it was easier to avoid signs of modernity.

Ugo Gregoretti filmed *Omicron,* a science-fiction/boom comedy, in a real factory in Florence, although it is clearly meant to be about work at Fiat. In fact, the film opens near the site of the Turin 1961 Italian Unification Centenary celebrations, with the futuristic monorail and "Palavela" (a shortening of *Palazzo a Vela,* or "sail palace") in the background. With its soaring cement curve, this structure looks like nothing so much as a spaceship—that's only one of the film's delightful jokes!

Gregoretti explained the film's origins:

> *Omicron* was a film about the factory, or better, about
> Fiat. In fact, the basis of the film was a study of Fiat
> done by Giovanni Carocci that appeared in the journal
> *Nuovi argomenti,* edited by [writer] Alberto Moravia that
> analyzed the difficult questions of unionism within Fiat
> after the creation of a secret police force that spied on the
> workers. A few elements of the film came from a meeting
> in Turin with the young people of *Quaderni rossi,* Fofi and
> Soave. . . . *Omicron* was a strange example of a satire on
> manual labor in a big factory, with an alien who takes on
> the body of a worker. I went to Fiat, a little naively, to ask
> about using one of their factories for filming and obviously
> they said no. So I went to ENI [Ente Nazionale di Idrocar-
> buri, the Italian state energy corporation]. Hoping to show
> that public entities were more open than private ones
> they gave me access to a factory in Florence, the Nuovo

> Pignone, specialized in the construction of gas canisters
> for cooking. (Bracco, Della Casa, and Prono 2011, 120)

The same director later found an occupied printing factory, this time in Rome, in which to shoot his hybrid fiction-documentary *Apollon*.[5] Noted actor Gian Maria Volonté narrates scenes in which the actual Apollon workers are filmed undertaking negotiations, playing soccer in the courtyard or eating meals prepared by family members. They also reenact scenes dramatizing conflicts. Volonté also stars in Elio Petri's (fiction) film *La classe operaia va in paradiso* (*The Working Class Goes to Heaven*). Thanks to help from the Communist metal-workers union, Petri found an occupied elevator factory in Novara, between Milan and Turin, where some of the occupying locals serve as extras, working side by side with Volonté, who plays Lulù, a dedicated worker who gains a political conscience, strikes, loses his job, and is eventually readmitted.

In *La Linea gotica*, Ottiero Ottieri, writing in the voice of a journalist/intellectual, explains: "If narrative and cinema have had little to say about life inside the factory, there is also a practical reason that becomes a theoretical one: The world of the factory is closed. It is not easy to enter or exit" (Ottieri 1963, 167). Workers can provide documents, but they can't elaborate on them. Intellectuals can investigate. The *inchiesta,* a mode developed in Italy by thinkers such as Raniero Panzieri, following in the footsteps of figures like Simone Weil and Jean-Paul Sartre in France, became a cinematic trope, for instance, as I have mentioned, with regard to Pier Paolo Pasolini outside the factory gates. But Ottieri insists that art cannot come from the *inchiesta,* only from assimilation, and it is extremely rare to find a worker who is also an artist. "To work in industry and to speak about it is a contradiction in terms." (Ottieri 1963, 168)

Meanwhile many Italian companies produced their own

(industrial) documentaries, including scenes of workers in factories going about their daily routines, often accompanied by lively music. One can almost hear the director, an outsider, shouting over the sounds of the machines: "Go about your business as if we were not here." The same year as *Renzo and Luciana,* Olivetti sponsored a film titled *Una macchina: un'officina (A Machine: a Workshop).* The camera follows the construction of a piece for a tractor made in a mechanized Olivetti shop in San Bernardo (just outside of the center of Ivrea). Only two workers actually touch the piece as it travels along a sixty-five-meter-long, synchronized assembly line. It is transferred automatically to different stations by automatic controls. If something goes wrong, a warning sounds and a panel lights up to show the spot so that a human worker can come and remove the piece. But, for most of the working day, this line functions without a hitch. The conveyor belt has become the active agent, thanks in part to new techniques called "'feed-back,' 'computer,' and 'servo-mechanism,'" and as Frederick Pollock insisted in his *Automation,* automaton is not an appropriate term for this context. "It is necessary to differentiate clearly between production with the aid of 'automatons'—i.e. automatic machines such as automatic looms which are constructed on mechanical principles—and the entirely new methods of production" (Pollock 1957, 6). Someday, the logical outcome of such developments will be factories without automata, without humans, perhaps (as Pollock acknowledges) ushering in revolutionary social consequences. In his vision of the future factory, workers will show up wearing not smocks, but dinner jackets.

Now, obviously, tractor parts are not Olivetti's core business. Rather, the company was in the avant-garde with *la grande meccanica,* automation on a large scale, and this film was meant to help with training for technicians (and perhaps help serve as propaganda for the company at the same time), as it claimed to "substitute warm, lively images for the cold composition of a precise technical description" of a manual.[6] In any case, for the filmmaker, it turned out to be very difficult to capture the whole process of the assembly line and the total sense of motion. He could not achieve a full panorama. So, he was forced to resort to animation at certain points. The assembly line, preprogrammed and choreographed, is different from other forms of manual labor because of the fear of sameness that it engenders: a progression without progress. And in this regard, the *grande meccanica* that Olivetti was developing for its own factories, as well as for others, failed to conform to, and even threatened, the principles of freedom that undergird Italian cinema.

Perhaps access to factories was ultimately granted, albeit on a limited basis, to the boom comedies like *Renzo and Luciana* or *Il mafioso* because these films were not explicitly anticapitalist. They do not lead, logically, to a sense of destruction of the machines. At most, they might lead to a sense of righteous indignation at the inhumane speed of production. Fiat workers in Marco Revelli's interviews talked of urinating in the chassis of passing cars or in coke bottles because of the lack of breaks.[7] Olivetti gave longer breaks and adjusted the assembly line to human rhythms in modes that are still echoed in what is called "Toyotism." Boom comedies explore the awkwardness of Italians fitting their bodies to the machines and schedules of ramped-up productivity. Perhaps, because these films showcase modern Italians on screen, they cannot (by nature) be full-blown critiques. They end up simulating a form of consumerism, even if they do so without conscious intent on the part of filmmakers.

Another cut. As the siren sounds, women (and a handful of men) run from their identical desks, again, apparently

con
Marisa Solinas
e
Germano Gilioli

At the sound of the siren, the workers run from their desks.

conditioned by impulse. The long shot is from the point of view of, say, a supervisor standing at the front of the room, and the lack of depth of focus emphasizes the enormity of the space, the anonymity of the workers. There is something both aesthetic and comic about the sameness. This is not a shot that leads, logically, to the idea of breaking free of chains of industry. On the contrary, the regularity and conformity of mass production becomes aestheticized. The shot also makes an explicit link between the work of manipulating pieces with one's hands at a station on an assembly line and the work of manipulating keys on a machine with one's hands at a desk. This is crucial, not only from a sociological point of view and not only if we wish to think of a company like Olivetti that was producing machines for different contexts using machines and humans, but also more broadly for the future of "manufacturing" in Italy and the West. When this work, whether done predominantly by hands or by machines, is fully established in free-enterprise zones, outsourced, and moved beyond the borders of the First World nation-state, some express a deep sense of regret and want to see it return, with all of the problems such nostalgia might imply.

It seems impossible that Monicelli, in conceiving these two opening points of reference—the clock and the floor filled with identical workers rising from their desks—was unaware of two significant cinematic precedents. The first is King Vidor's 1928 silent film *The Crowd* (itself influenced by Walter Ruttmann's *Berlin, Symphony of a City*), and the second is the 1960 release of *The Apartment*, produced and directed by Billy Wilder. Both of these works, made in Hollywood, are set in New York. Both move from exterior establishing shots of skyscraper office buildings onto sets. They don't even try all that hard to make this transition seamless. After all, they are working with very different codes from those of Italian national cinema's entrenched realism. These sequences from outside to inside dislocate the viewer from one coast to another, from the "real" world of work to the set of a film, in ways that will be significant for a reading of *Renzo and Luciana*. Both films

Women doing product testing at Olivetti.

zoom in on one worker at his desk, but only after a deep focus, wide angle shot to exaggerate, as much as possible, the conformity and enormity of the accounting departments where the respective protagonists are employed.

When Vidor's camera later swoops down and navigates the room, we understand that the crane shot is impossible; it is purely cinematic. The camera would have to be much higher than the actual ceiling to gain the necessary perspective.[8] So we know on one level that we are in Hollywood, where the sets were open on top to let in the California sunshine. The same is true, by the way, of the variety theater where the forlorn Sims seeks distraction at the end of the film with wife, son, and an enormous crowd of extras. If we like, it is this displacement (New York = real office building and real work; Hollywood = infinite space, sunshine, and false work) and the fact that we both recognize and deny it that makes *The Crowd*

A crane shot of the office in *The Crowd*.

so foundational. There is no similar displacement or duality in Italian cinema, of course. Italian directors don't shoot this way for a number of financial and cultural reasons, but most importantly because of the tradition of realism and on-location shooting that characterizes their cinematography to the core.

In *The Crowd,* after the camera dips down from the "open skies" to assume a "realist" perspective, it picks out the protagonist, Mr. Sims, employee number 137, at his desk and writing on paper (this particular office has no machines other than telephones on the desk of the bosses). Actually, at the moment of this shot, Sims is not working for the company, but thinking up slogans for ad campaign contests, one of the only ways that he can aspire to earn extra money, since his whole wage scheme is mapped out in advance by the company and does not suffice for a family man, or a man who wants to consume just a few more products, or make a move to a nicer apartment.

Then a cut to a clock that reads one minute to 5:00 P.M. A cut back to the worker who moves with exaggerated slowness. Then a cut back to the clock as we see the big hand move one tick to the right, landing squarely on the five. As with *Workers Leaving the Factory,* this is a silent film, so while we do not hear any signal, the workers apparently do, as they scramble to organize their desks, minimally, and head for the door.

The sequence is copied almost perfect by Wilder, but with the voice-over of his protagonist, C. C. Baxter (played by Jack Lemmon). Baxter offers a series of statistics regarding his place of work, the accounting department of a large insurance firm in New York City. The shot is so visually stunning that I had it etched in my memory long after I'd forgotten the rest of *The Apartment.* It must have been wildly expensive and complicated to dress the set, even if the shot itself involved only a static camera positioned at just the right angle to capture the ceiling lines fading into a single vanishing point. The convergence of the lines and the perfect symmetry of the desks have a dizzying effect: office work = death.

Baxter uses a calculator (an American-made Friden), and he watches the clock so intently and frequently that the camera actually has no choice but to pan over to it. Working hours for this particular department are 8:50 A.M. to 5:20 P.M. (so as to stagger the crowds in the elevators), and at the sound of a siren, the workers get up from their desks and file out. All except Baxter, who often stays late, not because he is ambitious, he notes, but because he has to wait until it's safe for him to go home. This sets up the major conflict of the film, which concerns not the workplace, but his apartment, used by management at the insurance firm for adulterous trysts.

To arrange the schedule, Baxter uses a paper (analog) Rolodex and the telephone on his desk. The calls to company executives are routed through a switchboard by telephone girls, and on occasion, the call is for one of them, from a (married) executive who wants to meet in the apartment.

The accounting department in *The Apartment*.

Later in the film, a push-button intercom sounds on the desk of the head of personnel. His secretary (and lover) forwards a call from the missus. Of course, the secretary is able to overhear the conversation without being detected. When Baxter is promoted to the rank of assistant director, with a key to the executive washroom, the only machine on his desk is a telephone. And keep in mind, too, that the plot of the film revolves around the problem of finding a domestic space for illicit couples to meet.

I will return to these two American films, but for now, it is enough to note that Monicelli, whether consciously or not, refashions these sequences for Italy. Because Italy is not (yet) the scene of the "salaried masses" on the level of New York, the director cannot duplicate the opening sequence to take us into the workplace. But then, he does not have to worry about establishing shots that set up one city and then move to another one thousands of miles away with the snip of an editing blade: Milan is both where the film takes place (the setting of the fictional story) and the city documented.

In *Renzo and Luciana,* the camera follows the white-collar office workers as they pass through the main factory floor, ducking under an overhead conveyer belt that would carry partially assembled pieces to a new station. Here Monicelli gives the viewers a momentary glimpse of the heavy machinery: truly an alibi gaze! What Monicelli does not show us are bodies repeating motions alongside machines on the floor or along an assembly line. To be sure, in order to truly capture the rhythm of the working day, he would have had to make a different genre of film, as I have suggested.

Fictional narratives offer a different perspective, naturally. After several years away in a sanitarium, the narrator of Paolo Volponi's *Memoriale* returns to what is obviously the Olivetti factory of Ivrea (although the author never uses a proper

The accounting department in *Renzo and Luciana.*

unknown whom Monicelli cast after auditions held in Mi-lan.[12] The director was looking for a slim twenty-something with green eyes. He picked Solinas out from a book of photo-graphs. She appeared young, "the exact opposite of the nymph who discovers her old age at twenty." "Her image seemed per-fectly suited to the girl in a white and black smock who leaves the factory at noon and goes to the nearby bar for a *caffe mac-chiato,* a sandwich and maybe three pop songs for 100 lire in the juke box" (Di Carlo and Fratini 1962, 37).

Luciana is an excellent bookkeeper, as we will learn.

Another cut. We watch workers file out of the factory building and down a set of stairs. Monicelli's camera pans around the crowd and locates Renzo in white coveralls, and then Luciana, also "in costume," a stylish smock, like a run-way nun. As we will learn later, Renzo (played by Germano Gilioli, also a nonprofessional actor, actually the second-string goalie for Milan's soccer team) works for less money at the same company, never named in the film.[13]

2

Clocking Out

Piero Umiliano's pop-organ jazz serves as the background as men and women separate into two lines and maneuver through a labyrinthine structure in order to punch their time cards for the lunch break.[1] Some Italian factories in the 1950s and 1960s used mechanical punch machines or stamps to register in and out. Regardless of the technology, the simple gesture of clocking out carries an enormous weight for the worker and the scholar of the worker. It signals a shift in what it means to be a human being, what it means to cross the threshold to exist on one's own time.

The Lumières' workers do not clock out. Not yet, perhaps because the factory is still more like a family, where they look out for each for other, where the managers know their workers. Significantly, these workers do not carry their work with them when they cross the threshold. Rather, as Harun Farocki shows brilliantly in his filmic study with the same title as the Lumières' first film (*Workers Leaving the Factory*), they are immediately humanized by their natural gestures and by the "mechanism" of the arrival of dogs roaming around.[2] We are not asked by the Lumières to contemplate what went on (in this very factory: making the film stock!) during the working day, only how the camera captures the transition to "free time." Because the workers' bodies are not exhausted, the viewer would not see them as slaves or think about reform, let alone revolution.

The rat race: clocking out in *Renzo and Luciana*.

Luciana and Renzo clock out.

More generally, though, Farocki was concerned throughout his career with "de-valorization" as an element of capital's contradictory state.[3] Olivetti (and '60s Italy in general) served as a laboratory for technologies of calculating time. One innovation of the period in question was the linking of punch cards to the assembly line itself. Information such as the rate of production and the presence (or absence, even for short breaks) of specific workers could be automatically input as data and then transmitted to another part of the factory, linked to a printer or tabulator (a *riprodutrice* or *tabulatrice*) and retranslated into numbers that could be read by a human where the pay envelope (*busta paga*: Italians were paid in cash, literally in an envelope) was generated. It is easy to see, then, how the increasing automation of the system of calculation made it easier for the company to vary pay according to productivity (*cottimo*) for a given worker or a given division. Of course, all of this information is then also archived. Clocking in and out is no longer the social event that it is in earlier factory life. Certainly, the badge is more discrete and "smart" compared with the familiar analog gesture of inserting a card into a mechanical clock to stamp the time or a turnstile that triggers a number to turn as the worker leaves and enters. Perhaps the growing idea of microchipping employees for efficiency of control and to enable cashless purchases goes too far. Ultimately, the difference is not qualitative: a machine verifies the start and end of the working day, a tick or level or bit of digital code that registers "after work hours." But the machine says nothing about what these hours might entail.

The logical conclusion of this today is the full automation offered by the swiped badge or time-keeping software, perhaps linked to the bank account of the worker so that there is no need for a physical check to be issued and deposited. How convenient! In the very near future, chips implanted under the skin might serve a similar purpose (as well as facilitating cash-free purchases from vending machines).

Recent works on Italian autonomist thought remind us that, for most of the history of capitalism (including the transitional period under consideration here), laborers, or rather their bodies, repeated motions in a factory, often with loud machines in the background. There was little opportunity for discussion during the workday or after work. Most workers were too exhausted or had to travel long distances to get home, and so were unable to come together to think about forms of resistance, being virtual slaves. However, in "Semiocapitalism," Franco Berardi's (Bifo) term for present forms of work, such as digital, precarious, web-based, screen-based, and globalized: "The soul itself is put to work. This is the essential point of the postindustrial transformation that we experienced in the last decades of the twentieth-century" (Berardi 2009, 116).

Work now takes place in a highly complex regime of invisible, inscrutable, cellular networks. To paraphrase Bifo again, labor now flows into streams of information made possible by ever-more complex and speedy digital infrastructures. The hierarchy and paternalism of the twentieth-century factory have been replaced by a more generalized and invisible form of control that reaches into every fragment of time. The ideal of positive independence (think particularly of freelance workers, called "autonomous" workers in Italy) may be dismissed as a delusional fiction. The net could seem like a prison, but in *Postcapitalism,* Paul Mason wonders if collective ventures, new forms of currency, and sharing economies could provide a positive way toward a new type of human and a new economy beyond capitalism. In any case, today we might well hold to a distinction between workers required to be in a physical space for a certain number of hours per day and those who are mobile, or who "co-work" with others in designated "incubators" or shared urban apartments as work spaces, or who telecommute, or are unemployed or underemployed.

Although he operated in a predigital world, Adriano Olivetti both anticipated and foreclosed some of the complaints of his workers by his policies of opening up the factories, bringing in natural light and creating green spaces for relaxation outdoors. After stamping their cards, the workers leaving the Olivetti factory (not only in Ivrea, but also in other locations) were certainly exhausted. They may have used the term "slavery" to describe their time on the assembly line. It is unlikely that, like Fiat workers, they peed into coke bottles or wore diapers in order to stay on the floor for long periods, the epitome of disruptive time constraints. But they also identified themselves with the company: they went to the health clinic or schools or sporting facilities designed for them by their benevolent patron; in many cases, they lived in Olivetti-designed subsidized housing where they might even have made use of some of the products offered by the company.[4] Other companies, such as Pirelli, at whose factory Mario Monicelli filmed his opening, offered versions of these benefits, but no other in Italy was so all-encompassing, and none inspired the high degree of loyalty to the company name (of the father) as did Olivetti. The Fordism that Antonio Gramsci linked to "Americanism" (in his notes from prison) is a "new" historical bloc that works preemptively against resistance and crisis by rationalizing production, paying high salaries (which allowed Ford workers to become consumers of their products), and exercising control over the ethical and moral life of the workers. Ford workers were still Ford workers when they clocked out, and psychological aspects of this mode undoubtedly seeped into Italian factories. For now, it is enough to mention this comparison with Olivetti in passing, as it may be pertinent to think about "time away" from work (keep in mind that Camillo Olivetti visited Ford in the 1920s).

Contemporary Italy is grappling with a problem: workers in state offices have been caught punching their time cards and then leaving; or workers may punch/badge in for their absent colleagues. Even in private companies, workers have discovered ways to trick the time-keeping mechanisms. Italian

In *L'impiegato* (*The Office Worker*), men trick the company by punching in for a fellow worker who is late.

law forbids the taking of pictures or surveillance that would catch them in the act. The crisis has been addressed at the highest level of government. Then again, it isn't new at all.

In Gianni Puccini's *L'impiegato* (*The Office Worker,* 1960), white-collar workers try little tricks such as punching in for fellow workers who are late.[5] Once the company hires a new (lady!) boss, Dr. Jacobetti (Eleonora Rossi Drago), she installs a camera on the clock so they can't get away with this. But, as is typical for a boom comedy, her "American" ways of increasing efficiency and eliminating waste backfire: both she and the protagonist, Nando (Nino Manfredi), crack up.

The time clock doesn't lie, but in Gregoretti's 1969 *Apollon: An Occupied Factory,* a recently retired worker who had earlier refrained from any form of protest shows up in the factory with a question. During his working years, the voice-over

A retiree shows his paycheck to the head of the internal commission in *Apollon: An Occupied Factory,* with the time clock serving as a background for this pathos-ridden encounter.

explains, this man had assumed that the printing factory's *padre padrone,* represented by the internal commission (CI), would take care of him. He always clocked in correctly, but his monthly pension is 40 percent less than what he believed he was entitled to receive. He doesn't know how he can live. "Now you realize what the boss is!" he is told by one of the organizers. "This is why we're going on strike. Maybe something can be done." As I have noted, this is not a comedy, but a rather particular documentary. We are to take the retiree's fate as emblematic. It is one of the issues that both the union and the internal factory commission tried to negotiate with the bosses, but to no avail. Hence, the strike is the only means of protest available. During the strike, the managers try to keep things going with scabs, but the paper keeps getting caught, almost as if the machines are conspiring against them, whereas the regular workers, when they occupy the factory, caress and clean the idle printers.

Workers entering a typesetting factory in Milan stamp their time cards in Ottiero Ottieri's novel *Tempi stretti* (literally "tight time," but more idiomatically, "sped up" or "on the clock"). Interestingly, Ottieri describes the crossing of the threshold in acoustical terms as "a tick, an acute sound, a trill" (Ottieri 1957, 23). During the lunch break, some return home, but for those who live too far away, there are food stalls in the piazza near the factory. In the evening, a man plays the accordion and some workers linger. Ottieri even describes what sound like quasi-situationist moments of escape, of interruption and difference. His young protagonist, Emma, has made a friend, in spite of obstacles like the factory being too noisy for talking and the different shops being so spread out that the workers have difficulty maintaining connections. During the lunch break:

> The two girls walked, arriving at a round piazza with crisscrossing tram wires overhead, surrounded by sickly trees and filled with colored signage: arrows, traffic lights, white stripes on the road. It was almost beautiful. An open area. They turned back at the sound of the first warning siren. (Ottieri 1957, 40; translation mine)[6]

This passage describes a real space, to be sure. In fact, Ottieri is scrupulous in his descriptions—even if telegraphic—of the new geography of Milan, with its inner rings and its growing outskirts. Interestingly, as with the film *Apollon*, the factory in *Tempi stretti* produces text mechanically: it is a printing plant.[7] To be effective operators of the machines after they clock in, the workers should/could not read the text itself. Their motions must be indifferent to the content of the publications, or they will be unable to operate as machines themselves.

Even white-collar workers clock in and out. In Ermanno Olmi's 1961 cinematic meditation on work in a Milan company, *Il posto* ("the job," but also "the place," significantly), one of the newly-hired clerks arrives just as his name is being called a second time. "Good thing you're not on the clock yet or you'd have punched in late," explains the manager. Could this be an echo of the opening scene in Vittorio De Sica's *Bicycle Thieves* (1948), where a representative from the neighborhood employment office has to call out Antonio Ricci's name twice for the poster-hanging job that requires a bicycle before he responds? Ricci's apparent disinterest is part of De Sica's attempt to paint him as self-involved, rather than the kind of immediately sympathetic character that might arouse empathy in a viewer, as has been noted by various critics of that canonical neorealist film. Ricci's melancholia and self-pity led some on the far left to critique the lack of any sense of class composition in *Bicycle Thieves*.

Of course, once workers are physically present, anything can happen. As we focus in on Sims in King Vidor's *The Crowd* (1928), we see that he is not working for the company. Instead, he is brainstorming names for a new fuel in a newspaper contest. We would not know about his stealing of company time without the close up, that shot following the swooping crane sequence that both picks him out of the crowd and reminds us that he is part of it.

Michel de Certeau introduced *la perruque,* a small theft of time, as a particular "tactic" in which the worker's own work is performed at the place of employment under the disguise of work for the boss. Nothing of physical value is stolen; what is taken advantage of is time, money in the form of productivity. De Certeau further defines *la perruque* by saying:

> It differs from absenteeism in that the worker is offi-
> cially on the job. *La perruque* may be as simple a matter
> as a secretary's writing a love letter on "company time"
> or as complex as a cabinetmaker's "borrowing" a lathe to
> make a piece of furniture for his living room. (de Certeau
> 1984, 25)

The worker diverts time away from producing profit for his or her employer and instead uses it for his or her own enjoyment, for activities that are "free, creative, and precisely not directed toward profit" (de Certeau 1984, 25). Everyday life, for de Certeau, is made up of "clever tricks, knowing how to get away with things" (xix).

During the '60s in Italy, there was an interesting point of intersection or possibly a conflict between the time clock and piecework, *cottimo.* The former is regulated by the "tick" of a machine. The latter is a calculation of productivity or an aspiration that gave rise to a series of conflicts. The base salary indicates the number of hours spent in the factory (with a speed of productivity established by a timekeeper). The *cottimo* indicates the number of items produced, so it may be fundamentally different from the first. Sometimes during this period, when the *cottimo* gets established, the base salary is lowered. In any case, I want to think of it as a measure of objects that is askew from or in contradistinction to the measure of time. As Paolo Volponi notes in *Memoriale,* when the factory owners decide to institute a total or universal *cottimo,* the workers react immediately by slowing productivity.

By their logic, anyone who produces more than they might without the rules in place is putting themselves in a situation of obvious exploitation, and what is particularly contradictory is that each individual fears that his share of the pie will be diminished because of the slow work of less productive colleagues (especially the women in the factory).

The factory owners could more easily intervene at the level of the chronometer (speed of production) and could manipulate paychecks by adding or subtracting *cottimo* more easily than they could influence salaries or the length of the working day. For their part, the workers could speed up or slow down or occupy the factory rather than punching out at the end of the work day. They could choose to caress the machine, as they do in Apollon, or to break them, or to perversely adapt their own bodies to fit them. Elio Petri's *The Working Class Goes to Heaven* follows a factory worker, Lulù, played by Gian Maria Volonté. Each morning a recorded voice instructs the workers: "Treat the machine that has been entrusted to you with love. . . . Your safety depends on your relationship with your machine. Respect 'her' [since in Italian, *macchina* is feminine] needs!" In the factory, Lulù cuts off pieces of metal tubing, coordinating between his foot on a pedal and his hand on a lever. Petri films him as he teaches some new southerners who have just arrived, so we have an alibi for the close-ups of repetitive actions. As I noted with respect to Luigi Pirandello's critique of filming as mechanical, Lulù explains that their work could be done by simians, in case we needed confirmation. But he doesn't mind: he's productive precisely because he assimilates his body to the machine. It is only the students and party members outside who label Lulù as a victim of inhumane rhythms. The sequence is long. By the time Petri breaks, sending the workers to lunch at the cafeteria, we've already had enough. We viewers of this film are tired.

In any case, at the film's beginning, some workers see their primary struggle as that between the wages and *cottimo*. This struggle could be worked out through the worker's assemblies and the trade unions. Some want a full strike until they have achieved "less work for more pay," while others feel that "reasoned" strikes lasting two hours will help them achieve better working conditions. Some workers want to destroy the factory and, with this, revolutionize the time of the working class, and still others have lost their minds and no longer work at all.

Once set in motion, Lulù cannot stop working (a filmic trope that finds its origin in Charlie Chaplin's *Modern Times*). He is tied to the machine of superproductivity, but it ends up blowing apart because he is no Stakhanov. As Mauro Resmini argues, he is less a figure of labor than an authentic pervert who can take pleasure only in what the Other, the factory owner, wants (more production).[8] He shows a new worker how to save time by seizing a metal piece while the apparatus is still in motion rather than waiting for it to stop. Time saved is money earned until Lulù loses a finger (the sexual metaphor is on the surface, not deeply buried). Lacking a digit, he can still return to the factory, where he is subjected to absurd psychological testing that Petri parodies with great fervor. Declared fit and back at his machine, Lulù's "strategy," if that's the right word, is this: Since factory labor is our life, why not work all the time, even Sundays? And why not bring in children and women as well? In the film's context, this is the most logical proposal of all made by the workers.

After being fired for protesting with the students and destroying property, Lulù is once again rehired thanks to the compromises negotiated with management by the assembly of workers. Order is restored. This time, however, there is no extra pay for piecework and no chance for "self-determination" on the shop floor. The agitators have now been assigned to the classic assembly line (the place of the least amount of skill). Here, they are arranged in a line, side by side, no longer specialized, and bound to a collective tempo (as opposed to working at their own stations, and thus able to work more slowly by choice). It seems clear that this "demotion" to an ever-more alienating situation is a punishment for agitation, and the pessimistic link between the factory and the asylum suggests that the workers are now "dead" (e.g., in heaven ... or hell).

Petri's film is neither a comedy nor a manifesto for the revolutionary movements of the period such as *Autonomia*. Precisely as film, through shot selection, sound, and editing, it offers an extremely rare vision into the factory. But this vision is far from transparent or linear. *The Working Class Goes to Heaven* posits the rhythm of factory work as a possible subject for a film (that is, potentially, a merely formalist and experimental one) but then undoes this by moving the action elsewhere and focusing on characters or plot. In other words, as a film, it first shows us smooth flow and then undoes that flow. Significantly, the film reveals the inherent weakness of the liberal critique of the inhumane speed of factory work—a discourse espoused by the students, the *figli di papà,* or spoiled children of the bourgeoisie shouting through megaphones at the factory gates. Nor can we justifiably take away a critique of machines as either displacing humans or dehumanizing humans. The machines and humans are linked in an affective knot, as we learn from the voice-over that greets the workers each morning.

Petri makes what we might call a Foucauldian analogy between the insane asylum and the factory, but then complicates any facile conflation of the two spaces, because in the former, where no work actually gets done, but rather only "time served," piecework prevails (the exmilitant worker, Militina, obsessively keeps track of his production and pay in a notebook). Finally, the workers are much more unified than under the various regimes of resistance, precisely in the uniformity of their movements, their mutual inability to hear each other, and the lines they form, just like little children marching automatically, martially out of the school, as Lulù notes. Petri gives us a glimpse into a space of production. We don't know exactly what it is the workers are producing. Lulù himself knows only that he is making pieces that go into motors that go into other machines located elsewhere. The forced interconnectedness of the human body and the machine is, for me, the one false note in the film. We don't need Lulù's monologue on the analogy: we know that the body and the factory both metabolize food or living labor and produce shit. We don't need to hear him boasting that he has a fully functioning machine "down there" after the company psychologist suggests he is suffering from symptoms related to his missing finger. More interesting are the aleatory moments when the physical and metaphorical machines break down.

By the late 1960s, workers at Fiat Mirafiori in Turin (a key site of *Autonomia*) formed human serpentine chains, disrupted assembly lines by tying themselves to conveyor belts, played card games during work hours, and marched from one building to another banging on metal, reproducing the noise of the factory. Reverse strikes, with productivity in spite of or outside of that demanded by the institutional powers, also disrupted predetermined production rates. But to be clear, nothing in *Renzo and Luciana* necessarily anticipates this kind of resistance.

In a sense, and certainly not consciously, a double contradiction appears before our eyes as we watch the shift change in *Renzo and Luciana*: if one is productive, then all benefit, but if one is *too* productive, one will not benefit proportionally, meaning one is being exploited. The workers immediately drop whatever they are doing; even one microsecond beyond the sound of the clock is too much. They separate, with men and women on either sides, and are forced through a labyrinth like rats. By cutting from inside to outside, where the camera is positioned directly in front of the factory gates, Monicelli performs a didactic function. We see that the workers have no allegiance to the factory, that they are themselves preprogrammed mechanisms that follow a preprogrammed itinerary. It is like binary code: you are either in or out, male or female, white coveralls or black smock. Typical of comedy, this is not a virulent critique, but an exaggeration that could actually end up reinforcing the normalcy of the process itself.

In contrast to the lack of camaraderie as the workers file out like cattle through the corral in *Renzo and Luciana,* it is possible that the factory could represent a space of belonging, especially for those southern workers who left behind a different pace of life. For instance, in his book on Fiat Mirafiori, Marco Revelli reports the following testimony of an automobile worker:

> Many people say it is difficult to get up at 5 A.M. to work in the factory. Yes, it's hard, but for me, entering the gates in the morning meant joining my team, and this made me feel alive, like myself. When I was a young man

they said I was a rebel. Well, at Fiat I was in my element;
people understood me. I felt good there. I felt good because I was surrounded by workers. I had all my friends
at the factory." (Revelli 1989, 53; testimony of "A. G.,"
originally from Naples, who began working in 1968 and
became a delegate in 1969; translation mine).

According to the accounts in Revelli's book, the period of solidarity of Fiat workers was brief but had a lasting effect. Several years ago, I attended a Christmas party at Fiat in Turin.
Upon presentation of an identity card, each current and former worker was entitled to a bottle of spumante, a panettone
(traditional Christmas cake), and a swag bag including Fiat
500 refrigerator magnets. Fiat employees mingled in a recep-
tion room over espresso and pastries or looked at the models
on the adjacent showroom floor. The atmosphere was pleasant and relaxed and gave no sense of the history or production of the vehicles, no accounting of, for instance, bailouts
after the 2008 financial crash. And there was no indication
for the future. Working for the company meant indulging in
this ritual, more as a way to mark the season than as a pledge
of faith to the company. I saw a retiree who had brought his
granddaughter, dressed up in a red jumper and black patent-
leather shoes, bored but resigned. Perhaps she'd work at Fiat
someday, but more likely, I thought, she'd go to university and
then move away, part of the brain drain, the *fuga dei cervelli,*
in search of better opportunities.

Given this scene from the present, what are we to make
of a scene from Olmi's *Il posto* (a film that critics compared
favorably to *Renzo and Luciana*) in which a recently retired office worker shows up in the morning in his old building, fully
dressed, napping on a bench until lunch time, when he moves

on to the company cafeteria with his former colleagues? In an interview, Olmi, who worked for Edison Volta, the Milan power utility, cited this as an example of behavior that inspired him to make the film. After all, his own biography was not unlike that of his protagonist, Domenico, who begins work at fifteen and looks forward to . . . a life spent primarily within the walls of the company, at a *posto fisso,* a job for life, a dream for his parents who wait for him every night at home, in a converted farmhouse in the Lombard countryside.

As part of his sociological research into the workers at Edison, Olmi was curious about the retirees who came back "because this was the only life they knew."[9] Unlike the documentaries Olmi made with the company's sponsorship, *Il posto* never mentions Edison (or any company) by name. As might be imagined, the reaction of the company managers to the film was ambivalent. There is no factory floor in *Il posto,* although we do learn that the fictional company operates out of different buildings in Milan.[10] Viewers might have known that the director got his training at Edison or even that they allowed him to use their buildings on Saturday afternoons and Sundays for filming. But, once immersed in the film, viewers would have experienced it as the story about the possibilities open to a young man, not an exposé of alienation at a particular firm. The workers of *Il posto* may be lonely, melancholy, or even hopeless, but Olmi's camera does not expose us to repetitious, hard labor and there is nothing overtly subversive in the film. Interestingly, for our purposes, Olmi manages to make a film about white-collar work showing only three machines: an electronic number board that lights up when an office has a letter to be picked up, a hand-cranked (or mechanical) calculator on a manager's desk, and a hand-cranked mimeograph. The first two appear briefly and would hardly be noticed by the casual viewer. The third plays a crucial role in its position as the clear symbol of the rest of Domenico's life. Its grinding sound is the last thing we hear as Domenico's droopy-eyed stare fills the screen before the fade to black.

Not a single typewriter appears on screen, although we hear them in the background in a scene shot in the hallway. Other than the final scene, the most machinic sound we hear is the click of heels on the terrazzo floors of the modernist office building.

3

Milan, circa 1962

If we wanted to read *Renzo and Luciana* as a documentary, we would simply shed all of the elements of the plot and replace all dialogue with the kind of "urban themed music" familiar from the genre of city films, and we would be treated to a visual introduction to Milan of the period, including factory interiors and exteriors and daily life, shots taken from passing cars, and unscripted and unstaged forays into the streets.[1] As it stands, by necessity, the camera, whether at street level, from the point of view of tram or car passengers, or panning from the window of Luciana's apartment, captures the city's boom: the subway, skyscrapers, middle-class housing and so on. It cannot do otherwise. In this regard, *Renzo and Luciana* lines up with Ermanno Olmi's *Il posto*, Michelangelo Antonioni's *La notte*, and briefly, Alberto Lattuada's *Il mafioso*, all of which document Milan circa 1962—a city skyline filled with cranes and a street-level infrastructure filled with holes. Olmi uses the construction site for a Milan subway substation at San Babila for rhetorical purposes: The job seekers Domenico and Antonietta (known as Magalì) are so self-involved that they barely notice a gaping hole in front of them. A construction worker yells at them in dialect, underscoring the lack of any collective spirit among the working classes in the modern city.

In the opening of *La notte*, Antonioni affords us panoramic views of the center. At first we might think we are in an elevator because we seem to be rising, but after we become oriented, we realize that we are not changing our location at all. Instead, the camera is swinging, ever so slightly, as if poised on a construction crane. Later, as writer Giovanni Pontano (played by Marcello Mastroianni) drives his wife, Lidia (played by Jeanne Moreau), through the center, we get a view from the hood of the car with occasional cuts that return us to the passengers themselves as they argue. Lidia also walks around the city. Antonioni achieves a high degree of "documentarism" in the driving and walking scenes (fashion, cars, shops, posters, and so on of the era). That is, we have to assume the camera is hidden because the scene looks so much like a documentary, yet we also have to acknowledge, if we think about it, that the camera must have been mounted on the front of the car, and then another camera mounted on another car looking in or tracking backward, following Lidia. Her existential wanderings in high heels take her to Sesto San Giovanni (Stalingrad), with factories in the background. Why? She used to come here, apparently, with Pontano before they were married. Perhaps she was trying to recapture some of the romance of their slumming days. We simultaneously enjoy an opportunity to take in the area from the safe distance of our theater seats. As Pontano and his wife move around, all of the passersby (who may well have been real people conscripted by the directorial team) are choreographed. We know this. This moment of recognition as (after)thought, or perhaps unconscious sense of a tension between documentary and stagedness, is particularly significant for the films I am discussing here. It is not exclusive, of course, to filmmaking in Italy of the early '60s. Still, the films of this period are saturated with a sense that the boom is something new, something worth capturing on film. Street life serves as a background to whatever else is going on: a background that comes in and out of focus but never disappears.[2]

Although it never ventures near a factory, *La notte* is also a crucial film for a discussion of labor and cinema in this period. In the second half of the film, Pontano is invited (along with Lidia) to a large party in a modernist villa outside of Milan owned by an industrialist (who certainly encompasses qualities of Adriano Olivetti). One of Pontano's readers approaches him. "What would you do if you couldn't write?" she asks. As is typical in Antonioni's work, Pontano doesn't respond, but the woman goes on: "Writing seems so artisanal [*artigianale*]. Putting words together. It's the only form of labor that can't be mechanized." Later, the industrialist invites Pontano for a serious talk in his office, filled with printing presses, machines precisely for mechanizing writing. The industrialist proposes to hire the writer on a permanent basis (again, echoes of Adriano, who patronized Ottiero Ottieri and Paolo Volponi, among others, even if the company was not always thrilled with their writings). He offers Pontano an *impiego fisso,* not as a worker or consultant, but a manager, a *dirigente,* to help develop better communication with the workers, to establish a cultural program, and to write a history of the company. Pontano (or, should we say, Mastroianni, since he is really "acting" as himself) looks amused. Perhaps he is considering the offer, but then he insists that he doesn't need the job. Even if his novels don't sell particularly well and he relies on his wife's money, he also writes for newspapers, he insists. The dramatic encounter between the capitalist and the writer as salaried employee is certainly rare enough. Intellectuals in the factory can never constitute a class, and Antonioni perfectly captures the ambiguity of this position.

4

"É sempre fattorino"

Standing at the back of the tram with her, Luciana's fellow accountants gossip and gesture to Renzo, who follows them in an Ape, the truck-meets-scooter manufactured by Piaggio that was so emblematic of the boom.[1] He's cute, Renzo, yes, the women acknowledge, but you can't change the fact that he works in the mailroom ("é sempre fattorino"). As we will learn, Renzo does not plan to stay there forever, or at least Luciana has bigger plans for him. In the Milan of Monicelli's *récit,* if there is not full employment, there is also no crisis of unemployment.[2]

Ottiero Ottieri's "diary" of work, *La linea gotica,* relates that mail-boys do crossword puzzles or read the sports newspapers. "They fill up their time waiting for the bell. . . . They are cut off from technology, from the various groups that form in the factory, from politics, stuck in the antechamber for eternity. They become gossips" (Ottieri 1963, 47; translation mine). Sometimes the mail-boys even spy on workers for the bosses, but they are themselves rendered invisible. Electrified technologies such as the bell help shape this kind of nonwork, as Rachel Plotnick notes:

> In fact, the more civil servants, call boys, bellhops, and
> other service workers were relegated to remote parts
> of the buildings they inhabited as part of a widespread
> social shift of physically separating employers from

employees, the more architects, electricians, and adver-
tisers advocated for bringing push-button communication into the personal space of those summoning their
presence. (Plotnick 2018, 49)

Domenico in Ermanno Olmi's *Il posto* also starts out as a mail-
boy. He is trained by an older man, Sartori. They sit side by
side at a small table. We hear a mechanized tone. The camera pans up briefly, and we see a board with indicator lights
signaling the office where a letter is ready for pick up. Then
a cut, which serves to separate the men from the machine.
Sartori ignores the signal and begins to talk about health out
in the countryside, a discourse that might have come straight
from the writings of Adriano Olivetti. To this point, Olmi's
camera has established a bond as Sartori teaches Domenico
how to survive in the office, in essence by self-humanizing
daydreams and avoidance of a Pavlovian response to the machine. But now the director breaks his neorealist frame. He
inserts another cut, not motivated by a diegetic sound or plot
or alibi-gaze. This time, the camera is apparently alone as
it enters the accounting room where Domenico will end up.
How did we get here and why? In the front of the room is the
hand-cranked mimeograph machine that represents Domenico's future.

Indeed, at the film's end, when a worker dies, a post
opens for Domenico in the very room we were shown, rather
abruptly, to interrupt Sartori's short monologue on the virtues of fresh air. Now the mimeograph dominates the new
workspace through its unrelenting industrial-repetitive
sound. It links productivity on the factory floor with white-
collar work.[3]

As a mail-boy, Domenico works in the administration
building, while Antonietta is assigned to another building in

The mimeograph, one of only three machines in Ermanno Olmi's
Il posto.

the city. We might well assume that the company has a factory
floor somewhere nearby. In fact, the only time Olmi makes a
connection from the interior to the exterior is during an odd
sequence when Domenico appears to gaze directly into the
camera and then, as we pull back, we realize that the alibi for
this gaze is his self-reflection in a mirror. Then we cut to his
gaze out of the window covered with raindrops, into a dreary
courtyard where we see what look like factory buildings. The
tone of the shot is very different from anything else in the
film. Certainly, in the context, it is very brief, but precisely
because it is inserted at this moment, if we linger on it (as a
still), we will think differently about the city, production, and

space, such that later, when Domenico does find himself in the main building for a delivery and encounters Antonietta in the hallway, when she opens the door slightly and we hear typewriters, we imagine women's hands even though we don't see them. Because it does not correspond with what we think of in relation to the building, it draws attention to editing as a form of displacement. It interrupts the smooth flow of the film and the moves from one location to another.

The low-contrast point-of-view shot out the window resembles the foggy, wintry Milan of Olmi's earlier fictional documentary *Michelino 1° B,* cowritten by poet and journalist Goffredo Parise. Here Olmi dedicates a disproportionate amount of screen time to the sea and sun of an unnamed coastal village. Made with direct funding from Edison while Olmi was still on the company payroll, *Michelino 1° B* recounts the story of a bright young boy taken away from the boats and waves (and the poverty of fishing) to a boarding school. In fact, Olmi shot in the two professional schools (Voghera and Pavia) run by the Edison Volta company in northern Italy. At first, little Michelino learns very simple tasks that will make him a good worker (*operaio*) for Edison, this time explicitly named as such, the company that powers the factories of Milan.

Michelino is not unlike the little Adriano Olivetti, put to work by his father in the factory; at least this is how we see it in the RAI (*Radio Audizioni Italiane,* called *Radiotelevisione italiana* since 1955; Italian state television) 2013 television docudrama.[4] In a flashback (after Adriano's fatal heart attack), we find ourselves in Ivrea in 1913 as the boy jumps through puddles of mud. His father brushes him off and leads him into the factory. "How long do I have stay here?" asks Adriano. Camillo replies: "As long as it takes to understand the factory so you can manage it when you're older." Obviously, the boy doesn't want to work. As Camillo leaves, we sense the boy's panic, but Adriano is soon set to work next to another boy about his age, Mauro. There is no class conflict or resentment here, just pure brotherly bonding. They will later become best of friends, and then enemies, but that's not crucial now. We see Adriano placing typewriter keys on a frame, laughing, as Mauro teaches him the ropes. The work is not exhausting; it's joyful. He drops a key: A, like his name. This coincidence provokes a smile. But then he is frightened by the sparks from a welding machine and Mauro runs after him to assure him all is okay. Cut to 1943. Mauro runs after Adriano. Sparks are again flying, but this time because Adriano is supervising the blasting apart of the brick wall of the factory to bring in light for the workers.

To be sure, such flashbacks and flashes forward are cheesy attempts to create a narrative of inevitability: the boy, the man, the factory, all wrapped up in a pretty package of wistfulness.

The viewer of *Michelino 1° B* watches the boy, half waiting for a disaster. Surely Michelino will run away, as does little Pricò in *I bambini ci guardano* (*The Children Are Watching Us*), directed by Vittorio De Sica and released in 1944. Perhaps he will witness some horrific event like Bruno in De Sica's 1948 *Ladri di biciclette* (*Bicycle Thieves*), whose teary face fills the screen after he understands that his father is stealing a bicycle. Or he might suffer some kind of physical or mental breakdown like Michele, ignored by his bourgeois mother (played by Ingrid Bergman) in Roberto Rossellini's *Europa '51* (1952). These doomed souls, wise beyond their years, haunt the screens of Italian postwar cinema, but in *Michelino,* there is no bullying or sexual assault at the hands of the boys or priests in the dormitory, and no industrial accident leaving him without limbs. Michelino looks a bit glum at times, but he finishes one of his exercises (forming the shape of a boat using metal wire) before all of the others in his class. This even elicits a vague smile from him.

Olmi makes use of voice-over, especially in the second part when the director explains to the pupils: "This school has a great task: it wants to form you into capable, honest and disciplined workers"("Questa scuola ha un grande compito: vuol fare di voi degli operai capaci, onesti e disciplinati"). Just before the boys are to return home for the holidays, a benevolent teacher takes Michelino aside and gives him (and the viewer) a sped up tour of what awaits him over the next few years until he will be old to enough to wear an Edison uniform. We are treated to footage of young men working high up on pylons or fixing junction boxes and so on. It seems as if Olmi could not find a way to convey the future other than to squeeze it all in as a slide show with extensive editing while the boy waits for his parents to fetch him. It is also the first time we find out that the school is highly specialized for training workers who will join the company. The final shot of the film, which should be the sun and the waves bathing the sides of the ancient jetty with the picturesque fishing boats and hearty villagers, never materializes. We never leave for vacation with Michelino. Instead, the camera lingers outside the classroom door where he has spent his first semester as a worker in training. The film ends abruptly so that the possibility of any other kind of future is foreclosed: Michelino, like Italy, like Domenico, has to grow up.

In *Renzo and Luciana,* Luciana gets off the tram right in front of the Pirelli office building, the tallest building in Italy at that time, a symbol of modernity, and the white-collar complement to the factory we saw earlier. Luciana's mother, father, and two young sisters wait in a station wagon. Why film the encounter there? First, Monicelli establishes with absolute certainty that we are in Milan, that this little film not only depicts Renzo and Luciana but also captures the portrait of a city at a moment of transition. The casual viewer today might not realize that the tram has taken us from the blue-collar to the white-collar division of the same company, or that that company manufactures tires for the vehicles that, like their station wagon, crowd the streets, as well as other rubber-based products for industry and modernization. Luciana's father complains about the traffic and says they would have been better off taking the train. In the boom comedy, the traffic, the generational divide, the large family crammed into a small car, and so on are all pleasant clichés that spark recognition and sympathy in the viewer.

Push-Button Jukebox

Renzo joins Luciana and her family outside a small church in a dusty lot outside the center of the city. In the background, rows of new worker housing are sprouting up. Inside the church, the family rushes toward the altar while a priest puts a coin into the jukebox to play the wedding theme.

This prop is a perfect icon for the boom comedy. A jukebox is a very primitive, mechanical sorter. It selects media (the 45-rpm record or a section of magnetic tape) and plays it. Each button on the interface has a different piece of information (one song) and each has the same quantitative value. It is like a calculator to this point, except that, within its box, the calculator also performs a series of functions secondary to these values, based on a series of execute keys. So, in comparison with other machines in use at the same time, push-button technology offers the user the illusion of choice without the anxiety of hidden elements that might outperform the human or take over our jobs or remember things we would prefer to forget. At the automat restaurant, the user selects food from a series of rotating trays but cannot customize the order by interacting with a cook. The technology is transferred to the "atomic kitchen" of postwar America as pure design: the suburban housewife selects an oven setting that has been preprogrammed into the appliance. Push-button telephones were developed at Bell Labs in New Jersey in the early 1960s, and at first they were hated. The very act of pushing a button rather

A priest selects the wedding march from a jukebox

than turning a dial or using another more old-fashioned interface may grant the user the illusion of saving time and effort simply because she feels modern.

Citing the Chilean biologist Humberto Maturana, Manuel de Landa notes that the machine button only triggers a series of processes; it does not cause or control them. Automated or "push-button" factories actually tend to function like autocatalytic loops. "Indeed, as late as the 1960s, a routinized, rationalized production process that generated economies of scale was thought by many to be the perfect example of a whole that is more than the sum of its parts. That so-called systems approach celebrated routinization as the crowning achievement of modern science" (de Landa 2000, 97). But such factories, conditioned by corporate planning, exhibit a limited capacity to grow or change. In contrast, computers might create networks or "meshworks of complementary economic functions" across different factories, leading to more dynamic nonlinear forms of production. Still, for now, de Landa acknowledges, hierarchical and closed models of production dominate.

The distinction de Landa makes between a positive dynamism and the static nature of routinization or planning is not necessarily applicable to the Italian '60s, but it is an interesting one to consider in the discussion of cinema itself as a machine. Push-button technology should be distinguished from the more generic sense of "automatic technology" used over and over in writing in the early '60s. For instance, an Olivetti theorist predicted a factory with a "central electronic brain," even calling it (in English) a "push-button factory," a factory commanded by the push of a button.[1] But this is not just a more advanced version of the "interactivity" of the jukebox. "At any time you can ask it [the electronic brain] a question and come away with the most astounding results, from enormous balance sheets of general accounting to the workers' hours on the production line." In this vision, different divisions of the factory send the electronic brain different sets of data every day to be entered by human operators onto punch cards that contain a series of numbers from 0 to 9, repeated horizontally on eight columns. Names (or words) are translated into numbers. For instance, the EG Lexikon typewriter is 10, the Lettera 22 is 12, and so on. The punch cards contain a special language that "men think and machines read and understand." The cards are filled in by women operators who have two keyboards, one with numbers and one with letters. They literally do a form of translation without interpretation for machines, a cognitive activity that could eventually be done by machines. Yet, in the language of the observers of the time, the work of "reading" the cards appears almost human (*operazione quasi umana*). Incidentally, while the documents I consulted in the Olivetti archive are typewritten, they almost all contain hand-written corrections or insertions. Writing

on a typewriter—something done by women—is most as-
suredly an analog process that combines machine and hand,
even after the advent of white correction tape. The archival
materials literally display the limits, but also the advantages,
of writing on a machine (whether mechanical or electronic)
before memory.

So, yes, data entry requires pushing buttons, but not in the
primitive digital sense. The fact that early computing is sub-
sumed under the rubric of "push-button automation" only reminds us, in retrospect, how difficult it was to communicate
the revolutionary nature of what was happening, even if, or
perhaps, even more so in the medium of (analog, narrative)
cinema.

In cinema, the push button functions as a bridge across
different spaces. Fred MacMurray, as the boss in Billy Wilder's
1960 *The Apartment,* uses the two-way push button to talk
to his secretary (with whom he had previously had an affair).
He has to be careful that he switches it off when he is talking
about his current paramour. But the secretary knows how to
use the buttons to listen in on his conversation without his
awareness. Wilder cuts back and forth between the outer and
inner chambers, between the different devices and listeners,
while the viewer hears both sides of the conversations, privi-
leged to an "omni-acoustic" effect. If this split arrangement
seems normalized for a generation raised on American television sitcoms, in Italy of the '60s, it was relatively new. The
push button is really more of an on–off switch, and in this
case, a very primitive digital component: in the off position
(the default), there is no communication possible between
one room and the other, so the secretary can gossip or com-
plain about the boss and he can be free to act unprofessionally
(in a comedy). In the on position, a channel of communication

Push-button technology for the (male) boss to communicate with the (female) secretary in *Omicron*, in which Gregoretti satirizes the rigidity of such positions.

is opened and the two parties are expected to assume their assigned roles.

So, while a push-button machine lacks the arithmological functions that are triggered with a calculator, the technology signifies modern convenience, and perhaps even the saving of user time more generally. That is why the jukebox in the church (no doubt a very real one and not a prop constructed or acquired by the director) works perfectly for the Italian boom comedy. The newlyweds are on the clock and have no extra money, and hence the wedding march is produced with a coin and the push of a button.

Hand on Calculator

After the marriage ceremony, during a transitional scene, Luciana changes back into her work smock. Then a quick cut and a close up of Luciana's hand on the keypad of a calculator. Actually, in this case, the calculator (oddly, not an Olivetti machine) is just an excuse to showcase Luciana's finger with her new ring. No casual viewer in her right mind would make much of this, but if we focus on this close-up, removed from the context of the film, it presents a whole series of suggestions.[1]

Almost immediately following this shot, Luciana removes the ring and slips it into a plastic box in her purse. This is the first time we fully realize that the entire rushed ceremony was meant to be kept secret. From whom? Not Luciana's family, but her coworkers? Why? Monicelli delays responding, merely positing the notion of clandestineness. Later we learn that Luciana's contract specifies that she must be single.[2] In fact, this was not atypical for the time period, and so, read in one key, Monicelli's little film, with its deferrals, appears like a standard liberal social critique of a labor law that allows the exploitation of young woman or constrains their personal choices. Yet a study of the film's *treatment* suggests that this contractual issue was not at the core of the idea for the episode when it was being developed. In an earlier version of the film, Luciana had not (yet) found a position. Without two salaries, the couple could not afford to marry. By this logic, if Luciana

Luciana's hand on calculator.

did find work (in another factory), then there would have been no conflict, hence no narrative and no film. Of course, and in contrast to the ideals of Olivetti, the primary reason for the company's policy is to prevent its female employees from taking off time for their pregnancies and childcare. So, why not employ (mostly) men, as in *Il posto* or *Il mafioso*? In many companies of the period, decisions about how to divide labor by gender were rather arbitrary as long as the labor was not heavy. There seems to be a more broad sense that the book-keeping division in *Renzo and Luciana* is a kind of model's pen. The head is a lecherous villain (the "Don Rodrigo" of the film), and he clearly wants to maintain the fantasy that "his" women are available to him.[3]

Carrying the realistic policy of this fictitious company to its limits, the company in effect employs women on whom it imposes certain restrictions and men whose civil status is of no importance. Women employees are either young and searching for a husband ("sooner or later I'll get married and then *buona notte*," as Antonietta says in *Il posto*), or old maids and widows. And even if this policy was actually on the wane by the time Monicelli shot his film, it certainly makes the fictional factory of the film's world a peculiarly interesting libidinal/gendered space. Since we have none of this information before us as we watch the film, after witnessing what appears to be a very brief marriage ceremony carried out during a shift break, we might suspect that Luciana is "in an interesting state," (to use an Italian expression) but does not yet wish it to be known, perhaps because she wants to keep working a bit longer. This is the logical path of least resistance at this point in our viewing of the film.

And within the logic of the film so far, if Renzo were to be fired, it would, in theory, be no great problem. There are plenty of factories in the city and he is a robust young man. Luciana has big plans for him anyway: he is attending night school to become a *ragioniere,* a generic term that translates as "accountant" but could refer to any sort of white-collar office job, such as that achieved by (the younger) Domenico of *Il posto.*[4] As such, Renzo could aspire to become the boss of Luciana's division some day. This would mean a higher salary, a larger apartment, and perhaps full possession of the appliances they have on layaway. A *ragioniere* would likely hold a salaried position, and Renzo could visualize his future (moving from a Fiat 500 to a 600 and eventually a 1100 or higher, a new television set every year, perhaps a plot of land and a lake cottage outside of the city, and so on, as in Ugo Gregoretti's *Free Range Chicken*). But he would probably not expect to move beyond a certain level of comfort. And for her part, Luciana would not become the rampant consumer or the wife of a true "boom" speculator. By showing us the ring and then hiding it, the film opens up this possibility only to negate it later. The series of positions and reversals around Luciana's status is crucial to the film, and they rescue it from being as banal as some critics believed.

So it turns out Monicelli has a very good alibi for the close-up, for the tightness of the shot. And yet, and yet . . . there is something out of place, something disturbing here. We are reminded, if we forgot, that the bookkeepers are not making anything creative; they are simply entering in numbers, a job that will very soon be taken over by programmable machines. The hand represents a form of labor on the cusp of its elimination by automation. The hand is the symbol of (manual) work, and so, when cut off from a body, it raises the specter of its end. The viewer sympathizes with Luciana precisely because she is attractive, young, and open to the world, all qualities that make her hand on the calculator a beautiful cyborg.

Flash back twenty years to Vittorio de Sica's *I bambini ci guardano* (*The Children Are Watching Us*). Cesare Zavattini's work on the screenplay was his first in a long series of collaborations with the director. It's a strange melodrama, to be sure, beginning with the title. First, there is only one child who watches, a boy named Pricó.[5] In fact, that he is an only child is already an issue because, during the Fascist period, the Regime encouraged large families. Second, the "us" of the title refers, we suppose, to adults who behave badly, or primarily to women, and in that sense, it suffers from a rather black and white moralism. One might also suppose that the "us" is the bad mother and weak father of fascism, the "we" who fail to exhibit heroism in the face of a choice. Yet the war is not mentioned, and this is far from being an anti-Fascist or a resistance film, although critics have certainly discerned visual and narrative elements that identify it with De Sica's famous or strictly neorealist works made soon after the war.

Pricó has returned home from a failed experiment with

relatives in the country. He is happy and gaining strength. The mother has returned from her failed experiment with her lover. The family has regained their harmony, or so we hope. In fact, it is Mother's Day. The little man and the big man are radiant as they sit on their terrace having a celebratory supper and laughing. Then a fade to black, and in the next scene, we see again an uncharacteristic close-up, a hand on the keypad of a mechanical calculator.[6]

A coworker reads written figures from a book. Pricó's father punches them in and pulls a lever, recording the sums on paper. It seems important that no new ideas are being developed here, only recording. No words, only figures that have no meaning except to another machine. Pricó's father is a decent

Hand on a calculator in *The Children Are Watching Us.*

man, and De Sica reminds us of this through his relationship to machines. His movements are as stiff and repetitive as any worker in a factory (only less strenuous, of course) precisely because his work forces him into this position; the work that he undertakes as a member of the intensifying middle class.[7]

After a moment, though, the camera pulls back from its tight focus on the hand and the machine to reveal a larger picture of the bank. There is a lot of chatter going on (again, something impossible in the factory, and this is a crucial distinction for theorists, especially around the concept of immaterial labor). While they are still on the clock and apparently productive, the father's coworkers give him advice about where to take a vacation. Yet there is no chance for genuine solidarity. Instead, the bank is a place of brief and superficial interactions against the kind of ancient marble backdrop that grants banks their gravity and authority. The father, as it turns out, is rather limited in his affective and creative thinking, and he can never truly meet the boy's needs as a mother would. Maybe holding a decent job, working the lever of the calculator, is the best we and he can hope for. De Sica plants his camera before a machine and a momentarily disembodied, machinic hand as they work together, a sign of the realm of possibility for being a grown-up in an Italy moving away from the war and toward the boom.

In Alberto Lattuada's *Il mafioso,* Alberto Sordi plays a mid-level manager, a chronometer, in an enormous Milanese factory.[8] We see shiny new Lambretta scooters—one of the most emblematic products of the economic boom—move along an overhead line. The chronometer follows scientific principles to regulate the flow, which must not be too slow or too fast.

About to leave for a vacation in his native Sicily, he skips through the accounting department (here populated with men) on his way to the office of the boss. The accounting

Baxter at his calculator in *The Apartment*.

Alberto Sordi runs past the accounting department in *Il mafioso*.

bodies are immobile. They are white-collar workers who are not physically exhausted, yet they produce mounds of data. *Il mafioso* is a boom comedy, and so, while it calls upon various techniques of comicality (from Chaplin's *Modern Times* onward), it is undergirded by a sense of anxiety about the time-regulation in the factory, as well as about the complete lack of autocontrol of bodies in Sicily, the home of the main character.

Following the typewriter, the other crucial staple of Olivetti is the calculator, first hand-cranked (mechanical), then electronic (still mechanical), then digital (the computer). The calculator is, at times, like the typewriter, gendered female (*calcolatrice, addizionatrice, la Divisumma*). At other times, it takes on a more masculine quality (*calculatore*) that belies its military origins. It's as easy to use as a pencil (according to an Olivetti advertisement) and takes up no more room than a telephone. There is nothing significant about the calculator in *Renzo and Luciana*, then, except as an alibi for the momentary display of Luciana's ring. But there it is: the basis for Luciana's days at work, a machine that she has come to know intimately. Luciana might have studied from a manual.[9] She might have learned to use the keyboard without looking (*digitazione cieca*). She might even have studied techniques for using her left hand (in order to leave her right hand free for writing). The calculators on screen in *Renzo and Luciana* are rather primitive for their time, and they do not include the advanced memory functions that were available. In short, Luciana does the kind of work that could very easily become automated with the advent of optical readers or scanners (entering numbers).

Calculators rolled off the assembly line at Olivetti's Pozzuoli factory, near Naples. In his novel *Donnarumma all'assalto* (*Donnarumma Charges*), Ottiero Ottieri gives us a rather uniquely detailed description of the process. *Donnarumma* is structured as a diary, beginning as the narrator arrives in a seaside town in the South with his wife to serve as personnel director of an unnamed company based in the North. He explains that the company has decided to build in the South for benevolent reasons, to help Italy. His words echo those of a famous discourse pronounced by Adriano himself at the opening of Pozzuoli: Olivetti has come to "create a new type of business beyond socialism and capitalism, because our times demand that we move with urgency beyond these extremes, beyond the social question as 'one against the other.' These terms will not help us resolve the problem of man and modern society."[10]

To be sure, Ottieri himself (and so his "character") did not undergo any technical training for the job. There were no formation courses in human relations in 1960s Italy. Instead, Adriano Olivetti believed that the intellectual would rely on his instincts to enhance the company and choose competent "dependents," as they were called. And then, as the narrator points out, in the future, with the coming of automation, all workers will have to become engineers, but in the meantime: "Why bother so much about the human qualities? Most of the tasks on the assembly line are still basic manual labor, even if specialized" (Ottieri 1959, 40).

Ottieri's narrator/diarist describes in detail the process of finding suitable workers for the factory. First, the requirement of literacy means that many applicants are simply not hirable. There is an interview, apparently to determine if the individual under consideration is minimally socialized. Applicants are asked if they go the movies. Sometimes they do, they say, but they do not like neorealism. There is also a test of hand–eye coordination. Some workers "are unable to fit the little iron pegs of the O'Conner reaction into a place filled with holes with only one hand and with the time keeper looking over their shoulders." "If we disassemble a Moede, a mechanism made of wheels, gears and levers before their eyes, they cannot put it back together or they will spend the entire time trying to do it. As a test of their hand–eye coordination, we ask them to use two levers to trace a curved figure on paper. They end up going far outside of the lines and puncturing the paper with the tip of the apparatus." The brightest among them do succeed, however. The narrator's assistant, known in the novel only by the initial S., exclaims triumphantly: "You see? The good ones this morning, verbally or nonverbally oriented, are spontaneously successful in the manual dexterity test even if they have never been workers; it's always intelligence that counts and we believe in the primacy of intelligence" (Ottieri 1959, 191; translations mine).

Like the actual Olivetti factory in Pozzuoli, the factory in the diary is no shack (*capanone*): it's a modern building by one of the most important architects of the times and includes a garden, an infirmary, a cafeteria, and a library.[11] Although the novel is primarily focused on the social context, there are occasional references to the product itself. Calculators are produced following a *meccanica di serie*. There are no deviations, no pauses, no exceptions. The narrator comments on "the monotonous and repetitive work of the machines that make millions of pieces for our products" (24–25), and he continues with a focus on "the symbol of this process, the specialized manual laborer between an artisan and an automaton, a specialized manual laborer, monotonous but capable, interchangeable like the very pieces he produces and yet attentive, responsible, with an irreplaceable technical knowledge" (26). The paint department is slightly different both in the forms of movements required and the danger of the fumes.

Ottieri's prose carves out a distinction from the Fordist

model. While the workers of the unnamed town in his novel are certainly happy to have the factory there, they are not the proud consumers of their own product. The implication, at least, is that, once they are subjected to quality control and packaged, the calculators are sent up north or around the globe, not distributed among the unemployed and backward southerners. Maybe it's just a matter of time until they too use calculators to tally their consumption, but it is more likely that the calculator is never going to become ubiquitous like the car, at least not until it is a computer, an essential commodity that everyone must own, but by then it will no longer be made in a factory in Italy. Nothing in Ottieri suggests we should read forward and backward this way, since he describes and narrates events day by day.

The diary is a form of accounting, but it is not intimate. It has a kind of logic that is not all that different from the serial production of calculators. In fact, Ottieri apparently wrote his entries in scholastic notebooks in the morning before leaving for the factory. The narrator displays in his flat prose the same sort of reasoned, slightly patronizing, but overall pleasant tone that he uses when speaking with the title character, Donnarumma, and the other locals who are desperate to get hired. For instance, he notes: "The psychotechnical exam is a good, proven indicator except that here we aren't choosing between potential workers suited for our particular needs: we're judging an entire people" (19–20). Here we find no syntactical or tonal distinction between the language of the dialogues and the language of the writing itself. Ottieri's prose, then, is mimetic of that technocratic language that Pier Paolo Pasolini saw creeping over Italy and insidiously taking over from dialects and older or expressive forms of speech, but it is also a creative manipulation of that technocratic language. Yet Ottieri does not write a parody. Instead he shows the pathos of the author who must be faithful to this subject and must avoid any temptation to write above or outside it.

At one point, the diarist goes down to the factory floor in order to help him better understand and enhance his ability to hire. While women do the *collaudo,* the testing of the final products, men assemble the calculators, although this division is not definitive since assembly is not especially heavy. In fact, some of the men in the factory had been employed before in metal-working (again, while it is not named, the Ilva plant nearby in Bagnoli is the obvious reference).[12] They tend to be much happier at the calculator factory because the work is not so physically taxing. Ottieri offers us a rare and detailed account of the assembly process, which functions in this way:

> I have to hold a *gabietta* [a little cage made of metal, like the cap on a champagne bottle with holes punched in and teeth]. I have to position it correctly in a holder on the bench. Then I line up ten legs in ten spaces, each with a number printed on top, from 0 to 9. I fit these into place by pressing on little springs.
>
> The pieces fit together only with careful maneuvering. Before they invented the holder, each piece had to be positioned one by one. Now, once the legs are in place, you have to remove the holder and substitute it, without moving anything, with a *dentiera,* a sort of cover box, that is slipped over to the side and then shifted toward the left, while you gently push the assembly holder.
>
> You then attach the case with two screws. The legs and spring mechanisms remain in place, and the numbers lean upwards. They have a spring under them so they move. This whole operation takes seventy-three seconds. (Ottieri 1959, 44; translation mine)

Although the process of writing is never directly discussed in *Donnarumma*, we would have to assume these notes to be hand-written by a male author, one who is perceived by the residents of the southern town as belonging to the management class (they call him *direttore* while he insists he is just an *impiegato*), and one who administers the psychotechnical exam but then spends time on the factory floor so that he can both learn how the work is done to enhance his position as personnel director and also then narrate the work to the reader without the awkwardness that would come from an omniscient eye. We are aware that the book we hold is a printed version of what was once hand-written in a notebook. In contrast, women such as the Signorina S. type up notes on a mechanical typewriter. The diary format underscores the hand; or it is possible that the prose we hear could have been spoken into a recording machine and then typed up (displacement in time). In this case, the typist is an automatic machine. If she makes a mistake or alters any of the prose, she is a machine with a glitch, a machine to be rejected, since what makes the product so valuable is its standardization (in price, construction, and so on). All of this machinic sense penetrates the prose of Ottieri's work as it also foretells of voice recognition software. If automation on the factory floor is paralleled by a division of labor around writing in the office—men dictate and women type—this has to reverberate throughout the culture of labor itself. The feminine itself is not absent from the world of office work, but rather haunts it, at the edges, as a presence that signals "automation."

The narrator of *Donnarumma* encounters and describes a serious moral dilemma. He feels he should hire those most in need, since the factory serves a social purpose. But instead, the company attempts to apply a set of criteria based on merit.

Ottieri / the narrator writes for other northerners, for literary types, but his prose almost mimics a corporate memo, as if he were trying to write an "American-style" prose. His visits to various parts of the factory are the alibi for our own presence there. He learns that the work under the chronometer is more difficult than he thought, and for this, he expresses respect for the workers. In essence, *Donnarumma* is a novel "written" on a calculator. This is not meant literally, in the playful sense that we might attribute to a Italo Calvino, for instance. Nor is it meant experimentally, like artist Vincenzo Agnetti, who "détournes" an Olivetti calculator, substituting number keys with letters that produce combinatory, enigmatic writings in his work *Drugged Machine.* Rather, in a profound sense, Ottieri's prose is intertwined with the object that Luciana touches at the beginning of the scene in Monicelli's film.

The early computer is called, in Italian, "electronic calculator," *calcolatore elettronico.* To be successful as a producer of *computers,* Olivetti would have to standardize components and move with ever-more determination toward a model of anonymous users, making transistors and other parts as cheaply as possible. Women like Luciana might have been employed, at first, to enter data that would then be memorized and recombined with other data. In Italy of the early '60s, an essential difference between the machine that Luciana uses and the "computer" is one of speed. The computer can compare calculations from the past with those made in the present, in order to "forecast the future" (Pollock 1957, 19). Yet they were stalled, in part because they could not easily move beyond the early days of the modular Elea and in part, they complained, for lack of a state/military/industrial/space complex. More practically, though, as Ettore Sottsass himself noted on the pages of the office-design magazine *Stile indus-*

tria, while the more generic calculator is made for a single user, "the electronic calculator is destined for collective work environments": "It necessarily becomes a focal point for the office and develops its own "personality."[13] The slip between the computer and the robot is easy to comprehend in this context, with a whole series of implications about technology, gender, and alienation to follow.

In computer history, the digital threshold is characterized by a shift from a reliance on tubes (valves), which draw alternating current (AC) from the electrical grid and convert it to direct current (DC) in order to power various appliances such as television sets, amplifiers, and even early computers, to a reliance on transistors. Glass tubes glow, like light bulbs. They are sometimes visible, depending on the size and use of a given machine, whereas transistors tend to be hidden within casings. Tubes heat up, requiring cooling mechanisms at times. In contrast, transistors amplify and switch electronic signals by using semi-conductive materials. In the simplest terms, current is applied to terminals on the material (the semiconductor) and flows out of another pair of terminals. Semiconductors grouped together are "integrated circuits." With transistors comes greater speed of processing power. Can the speed alone account for a momentous cultural shift, or are there other elements involved in the digital? Certainly, as Bifo (Franco Berardi) suggests, the digital leads to speeds that exceed the human capacity for comprehension:

> In the Fordist era, the fluctuations of prices, salaries, and profits were founded on the relation between the time of socially necessary labor and the determination of value. With the introduction of micro-electronics and the consequent intellectualization of productive labor,

the relations between existing units of measure and the
different productive forces entered a regime of indeter-
minacy. (Berardi 2009, 184)

Moreover, the primary function of computers in the period in
question was to store information (like an advanced filing system). The accumulation of more and more information is key.
But in time, as Nick Dyer-Witheford writes, "the real power
of information technologies lies not so much in their inde-
pendent capacities, but rather in the fact that their common
digital language permits the convergence of their discrete ca-
pabilities into increasingly powerful, combined, synergistic
technological systems." (Dyer-Witheford 1999, 23–24).

A scene from Elio Petri's *Investigation of a Citizen Above
All Suspicion* seems crucial to thinking about the transition
to the digital. The captain of the Rome political crimes unit,
played by Gianmaria Volonté and known in the treatment
and screenplay only as "the Assassin," has very recently been
promoted from the head of the homicide division, investi-
gating a murder (that he committed). He is getting a tour of
the vast paper archive containing files on the different subversive groups, from extreme right to extreme left. Position-
ing the camera for maximum depth, Petri emphasizes the
infinite amount of material on criminality meant to subvert
the stability of the democratic republic. But, as the archivist
explains, all of this is being entered into a computer and will
be reduced to a tiny footprint.

A punch card with the address of the murder victim is fed
into the reader. As the wheels of magnetic tape on the mainframe whirl around, the Assassin exclaims: "It's from America. The revolution!" Interestingly, then, Olivetti's strength
in this area is virtually forgotten in favor of a rather generic
cultural remark that was apparently improvised by Volonté

The vast paper archive of Rome's political crimes unit in
Investigation of a Citizen Above All Suspicion.

(or Petri) on the spot, as it does not appear in the treatment
or screenplay.

The address is cross-referenced against another set of information: names of possible subversives.

Earlier in the film, the Assassin calls an assembly of the
men of the political crimes division for an "American-style"
speech about how Italian values are being degraded by everyone from student protestors to prostitutes, from striking
workers to marijuana smokers. So, in an ironic sense, in the
film, the signifier "America" takes on the meaning of whatever
is tied to modern forms of control that are not indigenous to
the Italian character. Since this character is highly corrupt
and backward, the Assassin maintains, he has the responsibility to reveal it through his actions.

After the "American" computer wheels turn, Petri cuts to

"It's from America! The revolution!"

The archivist feeds data into a card reader.

a blurred image of "subversives" protesting with a red circle drawn around a man who lives at the address of the murder, Via del Tempio 1. After a few seconds, we realize that we are seeing visual evidence, a "print out" or slide generated after the computer has worked its combinatory magic. Another slide. Then another. The whole sequence is fast and disorienting. That is, Petri does not pull back to show us the larger context that links the mainframe tape reels (so very much like the reels of cinematic film that are turning as we watch the film, at least before video and digitization, of course), the punch card, and the display of the images. In fact, the slide projector is a secondary piece of technology, like a primitive movie projector, separated from the computer. To be sure, the trope of factory surveillance as tied to cinema comes directly from Chaplin's *Modern Times*. It is repeated in *Omicron* when the bosses watch the robot from the comfort of a large theater, or in the (post)boom comedy *Il tigre* (*The Tiger and the Pussycat,* 1968) when Vittorio Gassman, as the director of a refrigerator factory, watches the floor through a closed circuit television monitor on his desk, the only machine in the film other than telephones and a push-button intercom.

Surely, before they began location scouting and set decoration, Petri and his cowriter, Ugo Pirro, would have had in

The bosses watch the factory floor from a movie theater in *Omicron*.

mind a certain kind of technology for this scene. Perhaps they had knowledge of how punch cards worked in the broadest sense. A version of the treatment merely calls out for a paper archive, a computer, and a series of images of the "subversive" to be projected onto a screen.[14] These are the basic elements of an inevitable trajectory toward "the electronic," and so "the automatic," with all the ambiguity that these terms carry.

7

Marriage on the Installment Plan

The newlyweds, Renzo and Luciana, leave the crowded dinner table right after they've eaten. They escape into the bedroom, but it's terribly cramped, filled with boxes. As our eyes adjust, we recognize white appliances that they've purchased on lay-away. Now the viewer realizes, again, that this is far from a shotgun marriage. It's been planned and calculated for quite a while; it has been monetized, if we like. As it dawns on the newlyweds that they no longer have to hide, we simultaneously acknowledge that this is not exactly the first time Renzo and Luciana have already "behaved as a married couple." But how to "behave as a married couple" when the rest of the family is in the kitchen, just behind the door? There's no privacy and no space amid the clutter, so perhaps we begin to feel sympathy for them. Yet our sympathy can be aroused only if we aspire for them what they aspire for themselves: to live as on their own, without memories of the war, with cleanliness and efficiency, away from the prying eyes of the family (both the parents and young children, two generations that somehow instinctively recognize their difference from this "boom couple").[1] Renzo and Luciana have done little to deserve our attentions, however, other than appearing on screen in color, finally, after so many black-and-white films of war, poverty (both rural and urban), and precisely the porosity that we associate with the neorealist mise-en-scène: kisses stolen in alleyways, the intimation of intimacy between hungry bodies

Overhead shot of a Milan dance hall.

a more documentary quality, such as the historical reality of the exams, the subway, and contemporary Milan, the second part is focused on the interior life of the white-collar workers, "people who fall in love with the ashtray on their desk and protect it with their lives." He goes on to explain what he was trying to express: "At the beginning of the film the character [Domenico] is filled with wonder for every little thing—crossing the street, having a coffee with the girl. He is at risk of drowning in the world of work." But, with time, he falls into "annihilation, like the other characters, who have no interest in life." The scene in the dance hall signals his transition to the world of the *impiegato*: spent souls (*personaggi spenti*). These are the people Olmi met at Edison, and they might have been him if he had not found cinema as an escape. "Since they don't really participate in their own reality, they have no critical sense." These are the characters who surround Renzo and Luciana on their first night as a married couple.

A crowded cinema offers Renzo and Luciana another place to be alone in the company of strangers. This is the reality reflected back onto the screen: "In the dark movie theaters the little shopgirls grope for their date's hand and think of the coming Sunday."[3] Italian national cinema is replete with scenes of theaters, and often, the camera is positioned at the place of the film, picking out members of the audience who do various social activities but are very rarely caught in postures of rapt attention.

As they make out late at night in the company's Ape, Renzo and Luciana are surrounded by construction workers struggling to keep up with the demand for new buildings in a city that cannot grow fast enough. The shot captured here, then, perfectly encapsulates the cinematic "boom comedy": Italians facing their new social reality, a gentle critique evoking in the viewer an equally gentle sense of compassion for the newlyweds.

Renzo and Luciana in the "porous" Ape late at night.

9

Night School

The newlyweds (especially Luciana) talk very rationally and realistically about the future. They have plans: Renzo is going to night school to become a *ragioniere,* a white-collar worker, like Luciana's boss or like Baxter from *The Apartment.* In other words, he aspires (or perhaps Luciana aspires for him) to climb one rung on the social ladder, but ultimately, perhaps not more than one. There is a quasi-biological instinct in her future planning. Romano Alquati depicts night school as a *petit-bourgeois* fantasy of flight from manual labor, not a true escape from class exploitation. It might be better, he suggests with bittersweetness, for the worker to find a "nice little job where he doesn't feel crushed" (Alquati [1962–63] 1975, 146).

In fact, night school is essentially high school for those who, like Domenico in *Il posto,* had to leave right after the last year of obligatory school, at age fourteen. Night school represents, for Renzo, a promise that he will eventually find a regular schedule so the couple, assuming they have children, can function as a more "American-style" family. It goes without saying that this is very far from any kind of social disruption. On the contrary, it is also a social promise that he will not move backward. Like Domenico, Renzo will never devolve into the hypermasculine assembly-line worker who will rebel toward the end of the decade through violent clashes and strikes. He will never question the authority of the bosses or the State. His children will grow up in an Italy that is increasingly devoid of factory work, but they are very likely to attend university and perhaps to move up or out. Renzo (like Domenico of *Il posto*) is too old to become part of the wave of students that will attend the newly "democratized university," symbolized by student demonstrators in Rome in 1968. In fact, in 1962, when the film was made, the Italian Parliament introduced legislation for compulsory education until age fourteen. Beginning around that time, thousands of students enrolled in what was (and in a sense still is) a very patriarchal, nepotistic, and antiquated university system. But that's not Renzo's story.

Does "night school" signify, culturally, a kind of crisis of masculinity? Of course, we should make a series of distinctions in response to such a question: the steel worker (as we see him in Charlie Chaplin's *Modern Times* or Walter Ruttman's *Acciaio*) may be supermasculine, working without his shirt, sweating, and pulling enormous levers. Such actions are parodied in Elio Petri's *The Working Class Goes to Heaven*. Lulù also sweats and sets his work rhythms to his masculine urges. When Lulù loses a finger along with the tiny piece of metal that he pulls from the rapidly turning lathe, he is forced to stop working for a short recovery. After returning he is slower and more hostile. The company psychologist subjects him to ridiculous tests, holding up a finger and folding down the top joint, asking, almost rhetorically, "What does this make you think of?"[1]

A *ragioniere* named Aldo loses his job in Ottiero Ottieri's *Tempi stretti* because of his union activity. On the one hand—and we sense this through the narration—it hardly matters whether Aldo works or, instead, his fiancé Caterina is *sistemata*. They require only one salary to be able to move ahead. There is a short period of nearly absolute gender indifference in the narrative. But this goes only so far, for at a certain point, the author's voice interrupts to quip, "at the first baby Caterina will quit" (223), a line that cannot but recall the one spoken by Antonietta in *Il posto* that I have cited previously: *buona notte*.

In any case, night school opens up the possibility that the machine and man, linked together in their maleness, will part ways. Yet, lurking on the margins of Italian culture of this period was "automation," a word that, among other things, meant male unemployment, the lopping off of the psychological fingertip. So it can be argued that the early '60s represents a threshold in this respect: One possible end of the narrative is not perfect gender equality (that could pose a potential threat to the male director and viewer), but rather a different kind of outcome: men no longer working, but receiving a minimum salary from the patron state. Buildings in ruin. Call centers staffed by women working part-time. In this ending, the promise of a return to manufacture is dangled before men, tauntingly always just out of reach, while the threat of automation is repeated so often, albeit in slightly different contexts, that it begins to ring hollow.

Scholars have debated digital labor as a moment of potential liberation from traditional forms of salaried labor or as part and parcel of capital as a voracious and fluid body in search of new channels to settle into. Suffice it to say that all relations are ambivalent, but capital seems not to suffer from this particular form of potent neurosis: it goes wherever it can. Any discussion of the human and machine in Italian thought must make reference to the English term "general intellect," from the so-called fragment on machines in Marx's *Grundrisse*. To be clear, though, this text was not translated into Italian until 1964, in issue 4 of the influential journal *Quaderni rossi*. Its significance for critical theory and activism grew later in the decade, and then throughout the '70s and beyond, into the digital and post-Fordist ages. In the "fragment," Marx muses (prophetically, some say) about a future in which the central role of humans will be to supervise machines in the production of information. Already in his time, as he noted, inventions such as the automated cotton-spinning machine, the telegraph, and the steam locomotive were products of an aggregate social knowledge ("general intellect") contrasted to physical labor or brute force. At their most positively revolutionary, Italian theorists read the fragment to mean that, by coming together, the workers could seize the machines and decouple them from certain forms of capitalism. Others have read the fragment to mean that automation will free the worker to pursue creativity: the revolution is not violent, but rather technological. It leads not to anger or vengeance against oppressive masters, but to the worker taking up an easel in his country cottage during his ample free time.

For some, the fragment on machines is a truly astounding bit of writing. Marx distinguishes between early industrialization and later, when the worker "steps to the side" of the production process. Marx seems to have anticipated the information economy. When human labor is focused on supervising machines (of his time), knowledge becomes social. It is not difficult to translate these figures to today, but there is a risk that "general intellect" could be reduced to a meme. In helping to put the radical nature of Marx's fragment into context, Paul Mason makes the following analogy: "Marx couldn't imagine a web server. However, he could observe the telegraph system.... Telegraph operators were highly skilled but, as with the software programmer, the knowledge needed to work an electric key was insignificant alongside the knowledge embodied in the vast, cross-border machine they were actually supervising" (Mason 2015, 135). The relation between production and the social has the possibility to "blow capitalism sky high" (although it is still with us). Time not at work could mean free time for education and the arts. But is this the necessary path laid out for workers in '60s Italy?

Today "general intellect" circulates with at least two broad senses. On the one hand, it may mean something like the zeitgeist or epistemological paradigm of a particular historical/economic/technological juncture. And yet, on the other, the phrase is invoked to mean the collective (again, technological) and liberating knowledge of workers, perhaps opposed to the knowledge of the bosses. And, inasmuch as the bosses represent capital, they might be blinded or hampered by the single-minded pursuit of extracting value. The distinction I suggest above may be blurred or subtle, but in the former case, "general intellect" has a more passive valence: it functions more as a label to describe a generation ("the iPhone generation," "the precariat," etc.) than as a potential for collective action.

10

Milan Beach

On Sunday, Renzo and Luciana go to an enormous, crowded pool.

With this location, Monicelli is quite obviously drawing on the familiar trope of the beach scene, ubiquitous in Italian boom comedies. Enrico Giacovelli writes: "At the beginning of the 1960s, a visual and sonic bomb explodes on Italian beaches: the boom. That we are talking about an explosion, rather than a slow evolution, is demonstrated by the crude, coarse, sudden way that beach scenes are introduced into films with linguistic fragmentation, brutal opposition to the rest of the film, like futurist machines against the quiet of moonlight. The narrative rhythms of the films adapt to the breathtaking pace of these vacations. These scenes are pounding, frenetic, almost anticipating the modern video clip: intense editing, rapid movements, notable zooms, angled shots to highlight the 'ant-effect' from above" (Giacovelli 1990, 116–17; translation mine). On Sundays (or during the obligatory Italian August vacation), there are few class differences between the boss and the employees. Even though they share the same spaces even for leisure and conform to the same patterns, the workers do not join together to form a community on the beach. Instead, their sense of alienation grows, as exemplified in a scene near the end of Dino Risi's *Il sorpasso* when the camera (with the alibi gaze of Roberto, played by Jean-Louis Trintignant) moves through an all-ages

Crowds at the "Milan beach."

crowd of sad twisters at a seaside resort during the daytime: a woman with a cast on her leg, a little imp, a grandfather, all performing an expected ritual. Monicelli captures this same sense of isolation perfectly with his overhead shot.

Renzo leaves, perhaps to find a room for rent by the hour. Meanwhile, Luciana, alone on the "shore," runs into her boss and has to pretend to be single once again. She disappears for hours and the camera does not follow her. When she finally returns home, Renzo is waiting at her apartment, along with her worried family. Her absence does add some ambiguity to an already hazy situation: she's never done anything like this, as her little sister notes. Her mother and Renzo almost imply that "something might have happened" with that Don Rodrigo of a boss: quite risqué!

Monicelli's episode was cut from *Boccaccio '70* when the film debuted at the Cannes film festival. Some accounts suggest this was because the whole film was too long (although Sidney Lumet's *Long Day's Journey into Night*, also shown the same year, was longer) and Monicelli's episode was the most disposable. Others have written that the famous actresses featured in the other episodes (Romy Schneider, Anita Ekberg, and Sophia Loren) did not want to share the spotlight with an unknown ingénue (Marisa Solinas, who plays Luciana). Given that producer Carlo Ponti was married to Sophia Loren, there could be some truth to this version, even though (or perhaps because) they had their own series of scandals.[1] After some back and forth with lawyers and the festival director, Monicelli refused a large sum of money to officially withdraw and Ponti made the decision on his own. Whatever the reason, a number of directors (including Pietro Germi, whose *Divorzio all'italiana* [*Divorce Italian Style*] was one of the entries for the Palme d'Or, losing to *O Pagador de Promessas* [*The Given Word*] by Anselmo Duarte) and actors (Marcello Mastroianni, who was notoriously lazy and perhaps not all that interested in going anyway) boycotted the festival in solidarity with Monicelli. The event provoked debates. Jury member François Truffaut took the position that a film was ultimately the property of its producer, while other Cannes attendees argued for the rights of directors as "authors." Until recently, Monicelli's episode was available only in Italy. This is a miniscandal, to be sure, and worthy of discussion in another context.

Vittorio De Sica's and Luchino Visconti's episodes, both centered on stories of a "good" woman selling her body, were debated by the censors, although the film finally received the Italian film board's *nulla osta*. Following a law established in 1923, the board tended to pass films if they generally respected public decorum and decency. The film censors were wary of extreme violence and had forced Visconti to cut a number of scenes from *Rocco and His Brothers*, notably. However, their target was primarily sexuality that could threaten "public morality." Loren's exaggerated curves were extremely familiar in postwar Italy. Perhaps she was untouchable given her relation to the industry.

Films were not allowed to include scenes of apologies for

unpunished crimes; they should not incite hate between social classes or show cruelty or surgery. Hypnotic scenes were
considered problematic. The film commission, which decided
on the film's rating, included various public figures (often
Catholics) such as magistrates and the Minister of Tourism
and Entertainment, a new post established in July 1959 and
held by Umberto Tupini, a Christian Democrat of the Center-
Right. Earlier in the decade, voices swirled around about
Tupini's possible implication in a scandal involving the dis-
covery of a dead girl, Wilma Montesi, on a beach outside
Rome, not to mention that his own son appeared in a line-up
for one of the witnesses testifying about coke dealing in high
social circles (Pinkus 2003, 74 and 143). But the left has been
crying foul against the right in Italy since the dawn of time.
Nothing new under the sun.

In the other three episodes of *Boccaccio '70,* female *characters* manipulate the relation between feminine sexuality and
cinema to an extreme as their gorgeous female stars remain
available for the viewer's pleasure. Visconti's countess, played
by Schneider, is filmed indoors, in her lavish apartments, in
her bedroom, a protected gem on soft beds and in soft focus.
An object available to all, yet the plot ultimately confirms
the bedrock of marriage, the notion of a woman belonging
to one. De Sica's carnival worker, played by Loren, is offered
up to the random winner of a raffle draw. Her lower class status makes this tease acceptable, perhaps. Ultimately she uses
her cunning (a Boccaccian trope, to be sure) to preserve her
love for the one who truly deserves it. She is also a mother,
which redeems her and softens the effect of the bouncing of
her trailer as it travels over dirt roads, leaving nothing to the
imagination. Fellini's ultrafeminine model is played by Ekberg, playing a sex kitten, playing herself as Sylvia in *La dolce
vita,* a character inseparable from the actress herself. For all

that *The Temptation of Dr. Antonio* is a web of metacinematic reflection it is still a short film in which the voluptuous body of a woman/actress fills the screen.

It is worth noting here that even Wilder's *The Apartment* was marketed in Italy as a raucous film about sex, and most certainly not a film about office life. A poster populated with pin-up girls includes the taunting tag line "He [or she, as there is no pronoun in the Italian, only the verb conjugated in the third person singular] didn't know how to say 'no.'" *Boccaccio '70* was controversial, but ultimately it appeared in the cinemas, including Fellini's episode, which comments explicitly on censorship, hypocrisy, and morality Fellini's Dr. Antonio would be horrified by *The Apartment* poster. He would not see the film, and so he would not know that there is no sex on camera.

Monicelli's episode diverges from the others in hinting toward another possible scandal that never materializes as such. Let us recall, then, the twists around marriage in the plot, as these constitute a strong element of its comicality. (Did they or didn't they? Is she or isn't she?) The first mention of marriage comes as Luciana rides the tram with several female coworkers after their shift. There is mention of a certain "Marta," who ended up as a "concubine." "What's that?" asks another worker. Luciana explains with a certain authority: "It's when people are together without being married." Of course, this is precisely not the dictionary definition of the word. In fact, in these terms, Luciana herself was a "concubine" until her marriage.

Next, we witness the secretive and rushed marriage ceremony between Luciana and Renzo. The couple has been living "as if married" prior to the ceremony, so we have every reason to suspect the marriage is a cover up for a pregnancy. We are led along this path for several minutes. Luciana feels ill the night after the wedding. She faints at work and is sent to the company doctor, but she tells him she's not married and it's not possible that she's pregnant. We know she is lying about both. The casual viewer "gets it" and feels whatever she or he wants to feel. Luciana's pregnancy turns out to be a false alarm, and indeed, it is as she runs gleefully to tell Renzo in the factory that they are outted as a married couple and forced to leave in any case.[2]

Going beyond the surface of things, one might begin to have doubts. If the couple have known long enough about the pregnancy that they already began to purchase the appliances stored in the bedroom just off the kitchen, why the mention of termination only now? Why the complex mechanisms to keep the marriage secret at work in the longer term? In the film treatment, the "girl" (not yet named Luciana) cries. The idea of having a baby is so pleasant that maybe it would be better to give up, "if not the apartment, at least the appliances and furniture; maybe take a sublet." But, in the film, we never really get this sense of sweetness. A baby would clearly stand in the way of Luciana's plans, and in what we see on screen, she is rather determined, as we note in her explanation of the compromised position of the "concubine."

In another version of the film (outlined in the treatment), the wife tells the husband that she has gotten "her things," to translate an Italian idiom literally. The husband brings a bouquet of flowers to celebrate their freedom from this unwanted burden. He takes her to "park" on a deserted street of the outskirts of the city ("the modern hotels of illegitimate couples"), but the vice squad is making rounds. The husband and wife end up in the police station (another strange twist, since they are actually a "legitimate" couple), and they both lose their jobs. In the end, it all works out: they get an apartment and new jobs that will allow them to pay off their appliances, and once this is finished, "the possibility of being able to begin to think of a child" ("la possibilità di poter cominciare a mettere a mondo un figliolo").

In the film, to repeat, right after Luciana and Renzo are married(!), she shows signs of nausea. Her mother throws out a rather casual line, with Renzo and Luciana's younger siblings clearly within earshot, that "something could be done" with the help of an aunt. As it turns out, the aunt is not needed. Abortion did not become legal in Italy until the late 1970s, so why were the censors apparently not disturbed by its specter raised in this and other boom comedies? Were they not troubled similarly by Adriana's friend in Antonio Pietrangeli's 1965 *I Knew Her Well*? She shows up and brags that she's arranged "something like this" for women in trouble dozens of times. She wears her logistical expertise almost like a badge of honor. Perhaps this kind of language does not cause problems because the "something to be done" is ultimately acceptable to the male viewer. This "something" will take place off-screen, through a network of female aids and knowledge, and the male doesn't have to get his hands dirty. At worst, he'll have to pay and deal with some nagging. The boom comedy reminds the (male) spectator that this "something" is a woman's problem, while it also preserves her as a glamorous object on-screen, and if tolerance of female "problems" on-screen may seem hypocritical, it is precisely because women remain sexualized in comedy in spite of everything; censorship of sexuality is itself the ultimate hypocrisy. In this regard, Fellini's episode for *Boccaccio '70* is the most conservative and the most unimaginative of the group.

But then, do we really close off this logic so easily? If women can take care of things, if they can "do something" together with relative ease, routinely, who knows what else they can do? After all, when Adriana of *I Knew Her Well* is called into the police station to respond to a necklace stolen by a man with whom she had a casual sexual relation, the commissioner becomes frustrated with her equally casual attitude toward the law. "How I'd like to be your father now!" he scowls at her. Her own father, a farmer in the Tuscan countryside, has nothing but crude scorn for her attempts to make a life for herself, alone, in the big city. Various men in the film want to possess her, force her to work, or exploit her naiveté. The question remains: Is the gaze (Pietrangeli's and then ours) that follows the same trajectory of her body, from the window down to the pavement, definitively a paternal one? Or does she manage to escape this hold? Perhaps the latter, in that, contrary to so many other directors and their films, Pietrangeli does not here assert himself (or the viewer) in a "world without her," whether mournful or moralistically affirmative. Instead, the camera mathematically scans the distance from the terrace to the street and then the screen fades to black. There is no epilogue or alibi or male voice-over to put us all at ease.

When we get to the end of *Renzo and Luciana,* that brief scene based on Italo Calvino's story, the literary core of the film, the man and women behave as a "modern" couple. They will have children, eventually, we imagine, once they are settled, *sistemati,* and they have paid off the appliances and furniture. *Buona notte.* Or is it possible that Luciana might have some greater determination over her own future, perhaps precisely by turning to a network of feminine knowledge? For now, they both sacrifice and contribute their labor in order to move into the middle class that they both apparently desire with almost robotic conviction.

11

Shifts

For now, Renzo works nights as a watchman while Luciana has the day shift in another factory. She may not perform repetitive motions or assemble pieces, but it is almost certain she works with machines. Monicelli has no interest in showing us how she passes her time, and we may have even less interest in speculating about it. So what of their future? Would Renzo and Luciana have burned out or dropped out? Would they have participated in massive strikes at the end of the decade and the beginning of the next? Would they have joined in with social movements tied to the "refusal to work," or kept their heads down and tried to go on? Would their companies, like Olivetti, have managed to subsume or tame worker agitation by "offering, with a certain nonchalance, a superficial layer of technical bureaucracy for all of the mechanisms of compensation"? (Alquati [1962–63] 1975, 136; translation mine.) Would they have continued on in their paths with the assumption that things are just this way? Nothing in Monicelli's film permits us to think about a different future, since work of a certain type is what guarantees a continuation of the sweet middle-class conformity embodied in Renzo and Luciana.

At the time of this writing, the Italian government, and under the guidance of one its ruling parties, the Five Star Movement, is experimenting with what they are calling a "guaranteed minimum income." Those without jobs must

demonstrate a need for a maintenance stipend, and government agencies have gone to great lengths to stress that they
will check bank accounts and investigate hidden assets in
order to avoid abuses. The government has promoted their
program as if it were something brand new, without any sense
of historical precedents, when in fact, Italy has a long history
of proposing different forms of welfare or entitlements, including direct payments to residents of the South. The Italian "guaranteed minimum income" proposal is not for all.
Not even for all citizens (so it differs from what is sometimes
called "universal basic income"). In fact, it is a temporary stipend, closer to a form of workfare and subject to strict guide-
lines (recipients are expected to work for the state eight hours
per week and cannot refuse more than three offers of work,
something that is, obviously, very difficult to regulate). It also
has a limit of three years. Critics of the Five Star program
note that it might lead to prisoner-type work (roadwork, for
instance). The government rolled out the "high-tech" pay-
ment mechanism—a debit card that can be inserted into
machines—even before the proposal was approved. They
noted that it would force the recipients to spend the money
on basic needs, rather than, say, video poker. Rhetoric around
the program stresses the innovation of the card technology
over the socioeconomic changes the program might achieve,
perhaps a logical and rather pathetic end to a long geneal-
ogy that, at times, opened up the possibility that one might
choose to defer wages in order to develop creative projects or
volunteer or experiment. To live differently.

Renzo is riding his bicycle home at dawn and passes a row
of gas stations. He meets an old friend and explains that he
and Luciana have moved to an apartment in one of the co-
operative buildings. A cut and a few seconds of static footage
of the center of Milan, with the Pirelli Tower. The shot could

A poetic early morning shot of Milan.

be right out of a film by Michelangelo Antonioni: it's poetic, melancholic, depopulated, lacking the sharp focus that Monicelli uses elsewhere. What does it mean that Monicelli "cites" Antonioni at this point? The footage looks and feels different from the rest of the film. It could have appeared by chance in the editing room from a documentary by Pirelli. It's so still that it might even be a photograph, sutured in. Perhaps it is simply meant to imply distance and emphasize the fact that Renzo works in one part of the city and he has to cross the center to get home. I cite it, in any case, as an example of a filmic parapraxis, a slip. It means nothing in particular, but it signifies the machinic against the narrative, in the blink of an eye.

And then we are inside the apartment as Luciana begins to stir from the warm bed, where Renzo will soon settle down. In their movements around their tiny apartment, their adherence to their schedules for work and payments, Renzo and Luciana behave *almost* like automata. The bed, that elemental form derived from Italo Calvino's story, and their momentary tender glances redeem their humanity. Yet they are not all that human. There is nothing personal in the apartment, no art on the walls, no touches of bohemia or orthodoxy or passions or history. They are certainly not joyfully expending energy as a sign of their "refusal to work," as will the members of the Potere Operaio (Workers' Power) movement a few years on from the film.

Today, in concert with "general intellect," "flexibility" has become a positive of Silicon Valley and other industries that need to attract qualified workers. Adriano Olivetti's cafeterias with locally sourced food, green lawns, childcare, libraries, and summer camps sound like the amenities offered by high-tech firms that fight over the brightest coders now, and even hire the occasional anthropologist or poet to help write histories or enhance images. As I write, there are debates in the mainstream press and the angriest segments of the public sphere about the dispossession of precisely the worker on the assembly line that emerged in the early '60s in Italy. As the computer crept into the factory and the office, it began to eliminate error and to allow managers to exert greater control. Even in this period, gender began to enter into the discussion. Economists admit that certain professions that could be automated still function better with a human touch. These include fields such as teaching, nursing, and social work, but also more traditionally masculine fields such as Boy Scout leader, military commanders, clergymen, and policeman (Lekachman 1966, 233). The main distinction for Keynsian economist Robert Lekachman, writing just after *Renzo and Luciana* and focused on the U.S. context, is the speed of the spread of new technologies. He presents research to suggest that free markets will lead to better employment, at least in the present. When he asks himself about predictability of the Keynsian model for the future, Lekachman responds: "It is worth recalling that nearly three-quarters of a century after Watt constructed a working steam engine, most Englishmen still toiled in occupations little affected by the energy revolution. In mid-Victorian England, the largest single industry was agriculture and the second was domestic service." There were many jobs for the unskilled at that time, but: "Change in the modern world is quicker. It is not sensible to anticipate a sphere of computer technology at the majestic pace of the steam engine" (Lekachman 244). Big changes in work are coming, he predicts.

Surely, though, Renzo and Luciana do not think about such matters as they follow their daily routine and dream of their future. Renzo and Luciana will soon buy a television and watch, like all Italians, the *caroselli,* shown each night between 8:50 and 9:00. Perhaps, like Lulù, his girlfriend, and her son in Elio Petri's *The Working Class Goes to Heaven,* they will watch at the dinner table. In fact, Petri makes a brilliant cut from an uncomfortable close-up of the sweaty face of his protagonist at the machine to a medium shot of the sad familial trio with heads in hands as the familiar opening song of the *carosello* plays. Instead of watching the advertisements, though, Lulù ponders the nature of his work and his label as a potential ass-kisser. Even the child is too burned out to watch as Lulù turns to him, explaining that the bosses don't spend time in the factory. They're in Switzerland or America. And then the boy's mother complains that Lulù is too tired for sex. All of this as the blue light of the television shines on their faces that form a kind of reverse projection screen for the scenarios of consumption. And, as if this weren't enough, Petri introduces the *carosello* theme, sung off key by one of the men in the insane asylum in the background, while Lulù and his friend Militina discuss strategies for combatting exploitation in the factory. This interweaving of the announcement of consumerism as leitmotiv throughout the film constitutes a brilliant exaggeration.

Renzo and Luciana, and then with time, their children, would probably pay closer attention to the small screen. They would become familiar with friendly robots such as the recurring character Tic, an Italian version of Robby the Robot from *Forbidden Planet* (1956). In the sketch that precedes the naming of the product, Tic is a gift to the woman of the house for her birthday, and he solves various problems. A *carosello* made the same year as *Renzo and Luciana* features Tic doing all sorts of activities in the house, but when it comes time for laundry, he is brusquely shoved out of the way. A more beautiful and functional machine has comes to take his place, and it is revealed in the final seconds, the "coda" of the commercial: a Candy washer that is so easy to operate it renders the robot obsolete. The machine is an Americanized solution to the question of labor (saving) that feminists like Silvia Federici and Kathi Weeks will later analyze with great precision. Eventually, the fate of Luciana could be this: to save time by consuming products made in the factory where she worked before she achieved a status different from that of her husband.[1] The robot takes up a potentially perverse role in the family. He offers companionship to the woman and children during the day. But since he is also a pet and substitute child, what becomes of him, afterward? Viewers of the Candy *caroselli* will have formed an attachment to him, as they have with other characters, both animated and live. It is doubtful that they would link him to larger questions of factory automation, unemployment, and the future of work. In fact, he defuses tensions of that sort because he exists only in a very limited narrative, although he may haunt the dreams of Italians from generations now past and return only as pure nostalgia.

The story of Renzo and Luciana ends as it began, with the appearance of the theatrical curtain, disrupting the peculiar force of cinema momentarily, perhaps reminding us all the more that what is at stake is precisely cinema, and nothing more or less. Producer Carlo Ponti could have endorsed any number of techniques to divide one episode from the next, including, most primitively, a black screen. The curtain, however, reminds us about what cinema can do precisely as cinema. Cinema may serve us now as a central part of reconstructing different trajectories, albeit with gaps and overdeterminations. Naturally, we do not expect to arrive at a single point where all will be tied together, but at least we could imagine outcomes where workers might move in and out of structures, where inequality might be far less extreme, perhaps thanks to a basic income guaranteed by a state that does not act (only) as the "good father" (think Adriano Olivetti), but perhaps offers different modes of caring for different social actors or subjectivities. *Renzo and Luciana* and other films discussed in the present volume do open up unexpectedly to possible lines of resistance if we view them with an eye to fractures, sometimes microscopic, and with few exceptions, likely unconscious or unintentional. Such reasoning is subtle and surely a bit eccentric and possibly neurotic, and therefore entirely worth our consideration.

Notes

Opening Credits

1. In its early stages, the film was to have been called *Boccaccio '61* or *Boccaccio '62*, but because the producers worried it might not be completed in time, a date further in the future was used. The other episodes are by Fellini (*The Temptation of Dr. Antonio*), De Sica (*The Raffle*), and Visconti (*The Job*) and star, respectively, Anita Ekberg, Sophia Loren, and Romy Schneider. Monicelli's episode was the only one without stars, and this had consequences when the film debuted at Cannes, as I discuss later. Omnibus films were an economic hedge for producers, since, if one episode failed to capture audience attention, another one might well succeed. It was also a way to afford to bring in a number of important directors or stars without having to pay the kinds of salaries required for a full-length film. These films also allowed some room for experimentation. *Boccaccio '70*—the title referred to *The Decameron* as a frame for storytelling, but also to a certain bawdiness—was from the start always going to be a film with episodes about sex. It was born from an idea of Cesare Zavattini and supported by producers Carlo Ponti and Antonio Cervi. Initially they had in mind ten different stories (by ten different directors) set in the ten largest cities in Italy (mirroring the *Decameron*, at least in the question of the number), but the film's ambitions were reduced for logistical reasons, above all.

2. Monicelli is one of the under-studied but very prolific masters of the *commedia all'italiana* or *commedia del boom*. He directed eight of the early movies starring/named for the Neapolitan comic actor Totò, who also appeared in Monicelli's *I soliti ignoti* (*Big Deal on Madonna Street*), shot several years before his episode for *Boccaccio '70*. After *Renzo and Luciana*, the director's next film was *I compagni* (*The Organizer*), set in a nineteenth-century

textile factory where the workers decide to strike and undergo tremendous hardships. It was (and is) one of the only Italian films to take place in the space of the factory (actually filmed not in Turin, where *I compagni* is set and where modern buildings intruded in various possible locations, but in Zagreb).

3. Arpino was a writer and journalist who lived in Turin. Several of his short stories and novels were adapted for the cinema. Suso Cecchi d'Amico was a prolific screenwriter and actress who collaborated on numerous boom comedies and postwar Italian films. Monicelli's episode is partially based on a very slight but moving short story by Italo Calvino, "L'avventura di due sposi" ("The Adventure of Two Spouses"), from his collection *Difficult Loves*.

4. Camillo, from a Jewish family, married a Christian. He had to spend time away from Italy during Fascism. His son Adriano managed to obtain a baptismal certificate and was in relatively good stead with Mussolini. Adriano converted to Catholicism late in life, just before his second marriage.

5. Fulvio Trevisan, "Guanti di amianto," *Notizie Olivetti,* no. 23 (January, 1955): 23. In this brief article provided to the journal by an employee of Olivetti's health services department, asbestos is touted as a "miracle material" and "the best protection available from heat": "63.7 % of all hand injuries suffered by Olivetti workers could be reduced if each worker took proper precautions. Using the proper glove will help protect your hands." It became clear in the 1960s that asbestos fibers could cause injury in the lungs (its carcinogenic properties were not yet known). A company report suggests that, while there are no clear indications about the legal/fiscal responsibility of the industry, there are ways to "remediate" in the factory (Archivio Storico Olivetti [hereafter ASO], "Analisi dei sistemi uomo-macchina-ambiente," Luigi Pettinati, in 137 organizzazione, Lavoro, 304.003, Centro di psicologia miscellanea "sistemi uomo-macchina," 1968).

6. Among the histories I have consulted are Brennen 2005, Bricco 2014, Delvecchio 2008, Novara et. al. 2005, Rebaudegno 2016, and many more. The company was finally delisted from the stock market in 2003, after decades of struggles to compete in a global electronics market.

7. For "Programmed Art," see De Giorgi and Morteo 2008. Meneguzzo, Morteo, and Saibene 2012 offer a comprehensive account of the *Programmare l'arte* exhibit held in the Olivetti showroom in Milan in 1962. That exhibit also coincided with the presentation of the Olivetti Elea 9003, the first large-scale computer (transistor-based, and hence, by some definitions, the first "digital" computer). The first customer was Marzotto, a textile firm, which used it for logistics, payroll, and so on (see Ottorino Beltrami 1996).

8. The miniseries director, Michele Soavi, is related to the Olivetti family and the project was produced with the support of Adriano's daughter.

9. The most important exception is Romano Alquati, who developed a trenchant critique of how the veneer of social benefits, as well as the normalization of time-saving techniques and wage structures, worked to suppress potential worker agitation, to block workers at the company from developing a political or class consciousness. According to Alquati, around Olivetti, conflict was suppressed not outwardly, but because workers believed their work was made easy by the company's commitments to implementing automation; they felt they were barely working (the phrase *lavoro facile* had a great deal of purchase) (Alquati [1962–63] 1975, 137). More specifically, Alquati writes with great precision about the machines employed in some Olivetti factories, in particular the *giostra,* the carousel that turned objects around while workers remained seated. This mechanism (with a playful name, to be sure) was a means, Alquati notes, of preprogramming micromovements to extract the greatest surplus value from workers. All kinds of such activities and mechanisms were designed to hide class composition and the real exploitation: "The greatest error was that of the workers themselves, that is, following one motion with another, setting in motion the precise political mechanism that management had created with such mystifications" (Alquati [1962–63] 1975, 149; translation mine).

10. The Interaction Design Institute Ivrea (IDII), led by an English woman, Gillian Crampton Smith, operated from 2001 to 2005. The school trained students to use design to think about solutions to logistical, technical, and business problems.

11. For Olivetti and global finance, see Bolognani 2004, Brennan 2005, Bricco 2014, and Delvecchio 2008.

12. Doray, a psychiatrist who treated workers suffering from the effects of accelerated mechanization, offers a fascinating account of the transition from Taylorism to Fordism as "rational madness." The debate over housework as labor has been widely discussed. For a clear synthesis of some of the main points, see Hester 2017.

13. Ironically, American companies envied their European competitors. "Italian sewing machines and typewriters gave American producers a competitive battle as startling as it was unexpected. When Olivetti acquired Underwood, it sent its management experts to reform Underwood's *American* procedures, just as though the United States was an underdeveloped country. . . . . This was bad enough, but at least Americans could take solace from the argument that the embarrassing vigor of the European recovery owed much to our Marshall Plan and other aid programs" (Lekachman 1966, 211). Then, how to account for the Soviets?

14. For a variety of reasons, it is easy to understand why industrialists might not have wanted to grant open access to filmmakers. As Carlo Carotti notes, the Italian film-censor bureau was particularly harsh when it came to "less conformist" works, which would have applied to anything too heavy or politicized (Carotti 1992, 12). On the other hand, around the period in question, various companies began to see value in making documentaries to publicize their brands, and so self-sponsored films became increasingly common. Exceptions include Carlo Lizzani's *Achtung Banditi* (*Attention, Bandits*, 1951) and Eduardo De Filippo's *Napoletani a Milano* (*Neapolitans in Milan*, 1953). Of the worker as a possible subject for films, Carotti writes: "His very existence, while central as a figure and as a social condition, is also repressed and hidden: so he should not be the object of representation" (Carotti 1992, 11).

15. In June 2017, the neighborhood known as "Stalingrad" voted for a right-wing mayor for the first time in seventy years. Experts explain the victory of Roberto Di Stefano (supported by Silvio Berlusconi's *Forza Italia* party along with the right-wing *Lega* and *Fratelli d'Italia*) as a reaction against the center-left's proposal to build a mosque in the area. On a recent visit there, I was shaken to

see a large headquarters of Scientology, perhaps another sign of the end of an era of a certain kind of work and political struggles and the resignation of people to a higher and extraterrestrial power.

16. The film featured Piero Pastore, a soccer player.

17. See Rhodes and Gorfinkle 2011 for related issues.

18. In the film, the older term for this region, Lucania, is used. Visconti did some location scouting in Matera for a possible (unrealized) scene there that would have served to contrast with Milan.

19. Vodafone is a UK company. In Italy, service operations are slowly being outsourced, now to Contidin, the largest call center operator in Italy. Because Italian is not a global language, outsourcing to other countries such as India is not the usual practice. A dizzying series of takeovers and buyouts link Olivetti with Telecom Italia (and its cellular component, TIM) beginning in 1999. In a sense, this story continues to this day, even if Olivetti's name no longer appears on any mastheads, retail outlets, appliances, or stock markets.

20. An outmoded law still on the books in Italy specifies that banks and other financial institutions must produce duplicates of certain documents. So, in a scaled-down factory near Ivrea, Olivetti continues to make dot-matrix printers capable of satisfying this bureaucratic remnant.

21. Paolo Volponi was among the authors of an interesting document on the construction and staffing of Scarmagno preserved in the ASO: "Oggetto: Problemi della manodopera connessi alla possibile apertura di un nuovo stabilimento," October 4, 1965, 10.11 Centro sociologia, CRS 9. The company attempts to think about how to find new workers without disturbing the social equilibrium in and around Ivrea.

22. Vercellone argues that the development of the welfare state in Italy is rather unique because of the vast labor force from the South. Unlike other developed countries, Italy did not have to import workers from beyond its own borders during the period of Fordist growth. In one sense, Italy follows the classical model because consumerism rises dramatically in the South as well as in the North. But, unlike those of other nations, Vercellone insists, the Italian government understood Southern "underemployment"

as structural. Rather then providing unemployment insurance, the state provided southern workers with money in the form of stipends or disability pensions without verification. Internal migrations in Italy provided one of the key bases for worker struggles. The idea of the refusal to work that came to be crucial later in the decade brought together a diverse body of workers.

23. Ottieri, whose essays and observations about factories and industry were extremely well known, supported his family with a full-time job in personnel for Olivetti. After becoming ill, Ottieri moved from the North to the new factory in Pozzuoli (near Naples) and drew a paycheck for his work in the company while writing *Tempi stretti* during his free time. The novel was published as part of a series of the Turin publishing house Einaudi, run by the writers Italo Calvino and Elio Vittorini. It received mixed critical reviews. Calvino, for one, felt that it was too traditional. Ottieri's next novel, *Donnarumma all'assalto,* came out, instead, from the Milanese house Bompiani. It was nominated for the Premio Strega, along with Pasolini's *Una vita violenta* and the eventual winner, Giuseppe Tomasi di Lampedusa's *The Leopard.* All translations from Ottieri and Volponi are mine.

24. Unlike other notable designers, Sottsass was never an employee of Olivetti, but remained autonomous.

25. See Berta 2017 for an analysis of the advantages of a "foundation" for Italy, a country where workers were thought constitutionally ill-suited to factory work, in Adriano's mind. Italian business owners also complained they could not compete with their foreign counterparts who enjoyed support from state or military subsidies.

26. ASO, "Compiti dei servizi sociali," *Appunti e relazione di Paolo Volponi.* Fondo DSSS—Direzione Sviluppo Servizi Sociali (FONDO RISERVATO) / Attività di segreteria / Informazioni e studi sui rapporti tra attività assistenziali e industria, fasc. 199, p. 9.

27. Zavattini collaborated with De Sica on his episode.

28. Printed pamphlet, *Soggetto Boccaccio '61* (Rome: Marconi e Beccarini, 1960), 3 (Archivio Zavattini, Reggio Emilia, Za Sog, R 10/3/1, Boccaccio '70). Zavattini (and Carlo Ponti, the film's producer) seemed determined to push up against the culture of the Christian Democrats, who controlled the ratings and censorship of

Italian films. In fact, Fellini's episode is a deliberate conversation with/satire of these politicocultural forces.

29. In a letter to Zavattini, Vittorio De Sica summarizes Monicelli's episode-in-progress with these words: "Two newlyweds who can't go to bed together for work-related reasons" (Archivio Zavattini, Letter from Vittorio De Sica of May 3, 1961, D499/114, De Sica-Za 1961, DES-ZA). This was written before the film came out, so it may simply not be very representative of anything except one individual's perception of the crux of the film. Still, it is interesting to consider in light of the various twists in logic throughout the plot.

1. The Clock in the Factory

1. Typographically, the credits for *Renzo and Luciana* are remarkably similar to those of an American film, Frank Tashlin's *Will Success Spoil Rock Hunter* (1957), which play with the innovative qualities of cinemascope. This film, set in part in a Madison Avenue office building, satirizes white-collar work, but never shows us blue-collar or manual labor. It is certainly possible that Cesare Zavattini and Carlo Ponti knew Tashlin's film and adapted its style for the credits of Monicelli's episode.

2. See Harwood 2001, 108. I thank Courtney Fiske for the reference.

3. In the creation of *The Clock*, French artist Christian Marclay benefitted from the work of an army of assistants who scanned hundreds of global films and television shows for clocks (or, in a few cases, people making verbal reference to a particular time). The transitions were edited (digitally), again, by a team, and the artist created a separate audio track (with new sounds replacing the original, in some cases). *The Clock*, which has been widely exhibited, continues even after the gallery or museum is closed so that it always remains synched with "real time." In this regard, it is truly a "clock face" that advances with or without a viewer. Like a real clock, it consumes energy even when no one checks it and it opens up thought beyond the frame of its physicality (the projector and screen, the plug and flow of electricity).

4. *I compagni* was not well received in Italy. It certainly did

not find the audience that other Monicelli comedies did. Though *Renzo and Luciana* was considered "gracious" and "delicate" by some critics, it was also generally panned by the press as recycled "rosy neorealism," (a term used to describe films made in the wake of the more explicitly engaged neorealism of the first period), especially when compared to Ermanno Olmi's *Il posto* (*The Job*; 1961) and Vittorio De Sica's *Il tetto* (*The Roof*; 1956). The former I discuss throughout this book. The latter is the story of a couple of young newlyweds in search of a roof over their heads in Rome. As do Renzo and Luciana, they live with the extended family but want to be on their own, especially as they are expecting a baby. Karl Schoonover's reading of this film—focused on the theatrical posing that the family assumes in front of the pitying gaze of the building inspector—suggests a depth missing from *Renzo*.

5. He will also star as Enrico Mattei in Francesco Rosi's *Il caso Mattei* (1972).

6. n.a., "Una macchina: un'officina," *Notizie Olivetti*, no. 75 (July 1962): 27–28.

7. The argument about labor as a force that goes against bodily rhythms persists to this day, of course. See, for instance, Giorgio Cremaschi on the proposal to offer workers diapers in one of the last Fiat factories in Italy: "Il pannolone di Marchionne, *Huffington Post*, October 13, 2015, huffingtonpost.it/giorgio-cremaschi/il-pannolone-di-marchionne_b_8283600.html.

8. The director may have used dwarves to help exaggerate the size of the space.

9. The *qualifica* was a crucial notion in factory work in Italy. Essentially, it meant a specialization and promotion beyond work that required "brute force." But it is far from clear how or why it actually made any substantive difference to the life of the laborer.

10. A fascinating document from the Olivetti archives outlines experiments in the early 1950s with actually indicating the quota on the time card. This apparently caused anxiety among workers and did not lead to better production (see ASO, "Attrezzaggio," Fondo Archivio Ottorino Beltrami, fasc. 476).

11. Gustavo Colonetti, "L'uomo e la macchina," *Pirelli Magazine* 4, no. 2 (March–April 1952): 11–12, at 11.

12. Vidor cast an unknown as Sims, likely hoping that he would truly appear as just the man in the crowd. After *Renzo and Luciana*, Solinas managed to eke out a career in minor roles. As most all Italian viewers would have realized, the title of the episode refers to *The Betrothed* by Alessandro Manzoni, the very lengthy classic of Italian narrative in which two characters, Renzo and Lucia, overcome opposition to their marriage. In the film, Luciana's boss, who has a thing for her, represents Don Rodrigo, the Manzonian villain. But the parallels with Manzoni stop here. In Italy of the period, of course, factory women did bear children out of wedlock and shotgun marriages were often arranged. An unmarried mother plays an important role in the RAI Olivetti miniseries: she turns out to be a great illustrator who is not only hired by Adriano Olivetti for his publicity department in spite of her condition, but is taken by a young man (not the baby's father), who leaves his more "appropriate" wife at the altar.

13. Renzo is a *fattorino,* a mailroom worker or messenger, while Luciana is an *impiegata,* or office worker. The name of the factory is never mentioned, although it is referred to as a cookie or panettone factory in the screenplay and treatment. Perhaps Monicelli had in mind to film at Motta, one of the largest producers of Panettone. Interestingly, for our purposes, Motta was also on the forefront of mechanizing administrative services. In fact, they were early adopters of an Olivetti Elea 9003 (mainframe computer) to help calculate demand, warehouse storage, discounts, and shipping. See Domenico Tarantini, "Il 'Centro Elea' alla Società Motta," *Notizie Olivetti,* no. 78 (May 1963): 35. Monicelli *actually* filmed his opening in the Bicocca factory of Pirelli, one of Milan's largest companies. Pirelli began in 1872 as a tire company. It became increasingly diversified over time, and in 2001 a part of Pirelli was merged with other companies to create Olimpia, which also had control of Olivetti through the majority of shares (approximately 18 percent) in Telecom Italia, purchased by Carlo De Benedetti (ceded in 2007). The Pirelli office building, to the side of the Central Station, was an iconic structure, the tallest building in Italy at the time of its construction a year before the completion of *Renzo and Luciana.* "Pirellone," designed by Gio Ponti with assistance from Pier Luigi

Nervi, among others, appears in a number of shots in *Renzo* (and many other films of the period), as a recognizable symbol of Italian modernity.

2. Clocking Out

1. Umiliano was a prolific composer of boom-comedy soundtracks.

2. The Lumière Brothers' film was shown in a few different locations in 1895. Reviews stressed its "liveliness." We do *not* see exhausted bodies at the end of the workday, a theme that would become common in literary accounts of labor by Italian authors such as Ottiero Ottieri and Paolo Volponi. It is also worth noting that the Lumières made several films focused on the workings of machines, such as *Machines du Blé (Threshing Machines)*.

3. "But Farocki is ahead of such criticisms insofar as he explicitly thematizes the contradictions of his work's own productive forces. His withdrawal from narrative cinema is at the same time, in parallel with capital's penetration of the personal, affective and communicational worlds of the (former) worker, the exploration of a vast new world of (un/productive) images. Farocki pioneers new fields and forms of image analysis by scouting the emergent scenes of capitalist devalorisation—supermax prisons, combat simulators, maternity class and police training exercise, or venture capitalist negotiation session. Capital's growing interest in training and rehearsing, simulating and re/modeling every inch of the 'social factory' appears in Farocki's work as a project not of simple 'expansion,' but rather, I would argue, of involution and contracted social reproduction. Increasing precision is applied to increasingly unproductive and outright destructive functions. Work becomes an endlessly rehearsed performance in which nothing is re/produced but work; field of vision and field of fire merge with the gun/camera installations of the modern correctional facility" (Seymour 2010, 5).

4. Compared with North America or other parts of Europe, company-sponsored housing was not a major initiative in Italy, and no Italian company achieved the degree of control that Ford exercised in Dearborn, Michigan. Olivetti did experiment with housing

developments in Ivrea, in Pozzuoli, and elsewhere, but never at a significant scale. Fiat did not build worker housing, although the city of Turin developed whole neighborhoods inhabited primarily by factory workers, like Le Vallette and Falchera, although at times built far from the factories, perhaps in part to keep workers from meeting or to exhaust them. Today, more and more, the old worker neighborhoods are home to immigrants.

5. I am grateful to Paola D'Amora for her research into the location, the Roman *Istituto Romano Beni Stabili*, a private real-estate company formed in the early part of the twentieth century with grand social ideas. Elio Petri, who collaborated on the screenplay for *L'impiegato*, also filmed scenes from his *Investigation of a Citizen Above All Suspicion* (1970) there.

6. In *The Working Class Goes to Heaven*, a loud "emergency" siren like that on police cars sounds in the cafeteria at the end of the lunch break, leading to a mass exodus. It is a very disruptive sound-image.

7. Roberto Rossellini also filmed hard physical labor in a printing plant in *Europa '51* (1952).

8. Mauro Resmini, "The Worker as Figure": On Elio Petri's *The Working Class Goes to Heaven, diacritics* 46, no. 4 (2018): 72–94.

9. Ermanni Olmi, "Reflecting Reality," interview by Tullio Kesich, bonus material to Criterion Collection DVD of *Il posto,* 2010.

10. When it was first released abroad, *Il Posto* was given the English title *The Sound of Trumpets,* a reference to a line spoken by Domenico's father, who says that not even the sound of trumpets could wake the boy. In an interview, Olmi admits that, while it seemed strange at first, he actually liked the idea, as he saw Domenico as a spent character. Olmi takes his time, filming Domenico as he crosses the courtyard of what was a typical rural multidwelling structure, passes through the town square of Meda, and rushes for the train. In one version of the treatment, Olmi suggests that Domenico should arrive early, but he is intimidated by the idea of entering the waiting room, so he hangs out near the tracks. This does not appear in the film, but it is another indication of the fact that Domenico is a boy about to be thrust into the world of adults before he is ready. During the train ride to Milan, the director clearly establishes an alternative: another boy

is on his way to school and almost seems envious of Domenico, who would himself prefer to continue to study. Then a cut, and we watch as Domenico arrives at a modernist glass building (actually Edison headquarters, a few blocks from the iconic Milanese Duomo). The building still stands, on Via San Giovanni sul Muro, now occupied by offices of ENEL, the electric utility. As I noted, though, the company is never named in the film and the viewer never learns precisely what they produce (nor does Domenico, at least as far as we can tell). After attendance is taken in a cramped waiting room, the recruits walk single file outside, on their way to take the "psychotechnical exam." A man stops Domenico to ask what is going on. In fact, in the treatment, Olmi specifies that the recruits, each holding a piece of white paper (not seen in the film), should arouse curiosity as they parade along. The exam was shot in the ornate Palazzo Melzi d'Eril, via Manin 23, a little less than two kilometers away from Edison (about twenty five minutes on foot in real time). The Palazzo currently houses the Fondazione Cariplo, the large philanthropic organization of an Italian bank. Afterward, during the lunch break, Domenico and Antonietta walk past the construction of the new subway line in Piazza San Babila, which is not actually on the way to either building. Only this location is specified in the treatment and screenplay. Olmi definitely wanted to show that the city was modernizing and expanding. The open pit of the subway dig must have been quite a spectacle for the Milanese public, and it is a perfect background to express, once again, Domenico's timidity, as he fails to understand where to cross the street and leaves Antonietta alone on the other side. Indeed, in the treatment, he is ashamed as a traffic cop scolds him. In other words, Olmi scouted locations for shooting and took a few liberties with editing—perfectly acceptable and within the norm for a fiction film! In an interview reflecting on *Il posto*, Olmi confessed: "I don't have a solution." But then he asks, rhetorically, what the problem is with that. "We might say that it was the tumult caused by overnight mechanization of everything. I've always said: look at the people who live in contact with nature and who experience everyday some sense of equilibrium that leads to participation, some sense of balance." *Renzo and Luciana* never ventures outside the city, but in *Il Posto,* Olmi did film a short scene where Domenico and Antonietta run, laughing, through a park. Is that enough?

3. Milan, circa 1962

1. See Rhodes 2019 on the 1929 *Stramilano.* As John Foot notes (1999), *Rocco* was advertised as a film showing more of Milan than had ever been shown before.

2. These were the early days of live television in Italy.

4. "É sempre fattorino"

1 Like Olivetti, Piaggio was founded by a patriarch, Enrico Piaggio, in the late nineteenth century in northern Italy (near Genoa) and then passed down to his sons. What had been a company known for producing wood-based products grew to make vehicles and parts for the war out of steel, and eventually cars and scooters. Piaggio is best known for the Vespa, *the* icon of the boom. There would be no boom without the Vespa, it might be said. The Ape model developed in the same postwar context, in 1947. It was conceived for transport of commercial goods, but it was also used as taxi and city car. Like Olivetti, Piaggio was eventually taken over (in this case by the Fiat group) and it later went public. Unlike Olivetti, it is still producing (outside of Italy) for the global market. The basic form of the Vespa remains virtually unchanged. It is functional while simultaneously conveying a sense of nostalgia.

2. Compared with other European cities, Milan in this period does not seem to significantly distinguish between types of living situations. Some workers did live in communities called *coree,* halfway between worker housing and squatter sites. For these see, Foot 1999. Others, like Luciana's family or the characters in Ottieri's novel *Tempi stretti,* lived in the center of the city in cramped apartments. A good portion of the workforce at Pirelli Bicocca lived in the Lombard countryside and commuted to the factory by rail, like Domenico in *Il posto.*

3. Although the final shot and sound of the mimeograph

dominates viewers' experience of the film, it was not part of the original treatment held in the Turin cinema library, suggesting that Olmi may have conceived of it later or encountered this particular machine on location during shooting and resolved to incorporate it.

4. Adriano did work as a factory boy for a period of several years in the 1920s.

5. Push-Button Jukebox

1. N.a., "L'automazione alla TV," *Notizie Olivetti,* no. 43 (January 1957): 5. Also see Gustavo Colonetti, "Automazione: evoluzione o rivoluzione?" *Pirelli Magazine* 4, no. 2 (March–April 1952): 11–12. Pirelli Bicocca workers threatened to strike for higher wages in 1968, but the unions accepted a rather weak deal with management. Manual and office workers (like Renzo and Luciana) did form a *Comitato Unitario di Base* (CUB; United Base Committee). They were successful in gaining pay raises through a series of strikes and other actions, and they sparked action throughout the industrial triangle of Milan, Turin, and Genoa. Moreover, the northern CUBs also worked for pay equity for workers in the South.

6. Hand on Calculator

1. For more on the hand/keyboard/machine function of the calculator, see Pinkus 2017.

2. This practice was not as prevalent as it had been by the time Monicelli made his film, as he acknowledged, but it was still worthy of comment. The Italian government discussed at length to what degree such rules could be applied by private industry or negated by the state or trade unions; see Italian Parliament, Law of January 9, 1963, no. 7/ Divieto di licenziamento delle lavoratrici per causa di matrimonio e modifiche alla legge 26 agosto 1950 [Prohibition of dismissal of workers due to marriage and amendments to the law of August 26, 1950], no. 860: "Tutela fisica ed economica delle lavoratrici madri [Physical and economic protection of working mothers]" (Gazzetta Ufficiale, no. 27, January 30,1963, sintesi. provincia.milano.it/portalemilano/pdf/legge9gennaio1963n7.pdf)

3. In Alessandro Manzoni's 1827 novel *The Betrothed*, set in the early seventeenth century, Don Rodrigo is the thuggish baron who attempts to interrupt the marriage of Renzo and Lucia. In stark contrast to the situation faced by the characters in Monicelli's film, the RAI 2013 television miniseries has Adriano Olivetti stroke the belly of a pregnant woman in the factory. We see a figurative light bulb go off in his head, and he soon declares a year of paid leave for all new mothers with guarantee of reemployment. In Ottiero Ottieri's 1957 novel *Tempi stretti,* there is also a certain gender equity in the typesetting factory and particularly when it comes to work that requires a treadle or coordination between hands and feet. When a married worker is caught during a break with a woman, the managers offer to fire him and hire his wife instead so that at least the family will not starve. Emma, one of the central protagonists of that novel, is the only one of five children (the others are male) who works, and she is expected to send money home to her (southern) village. We presume this is because, in the South, there is nothing for her to do except be a burden, whereas the boys might at least keep up the family farm or fish. In Ottieri's 1959 *Donnarumma all'assalto,* set in an (Olivetti) calculator factory in the South, the narrator has to intervene in a family drama when one of the female workers wants to marry and leave the town, substituting her sister in her place. But the sister is not as qualified, so she is offered a position as a janitor, at least to start. She refuses because she feels certain that such demeaning work will make her unattractive to potential husbands. The family falls apart in a minidrama.

4. In *I bambini ci guardano* (*The Children Are Watching Us*; 1944), the father, Andrea, is a *ragionere*.

5. The film is loosely based on the novel *Pricò* by Massimo d'Azeglio; the name means "precocious."

6. In the screenplay, it is indicated as a "cash register." Clearly it is not the specific function of the machine itself that preoccupied De Sica or Zavattini, but the broader context of the interactions of the men around a machine.

7. Bankers and their calculators are (understandably) absent from Fascist propaganda films that tend to feature hearty and

healthy peasants working the fields or sober soldiers and tanks, or brown-shirted children lining up for their paramilitary exercises. When banks *do* appear in Fascist culture, it is often in relation to savings campaigns. For instance, advertisements were common featuring a child holding the piggy bank; or a bank might put forward images of peasants sowing seeds in a field for future yield. See Pinkus 1995 (esp. pp. 70–73 and 144–47).

8. The factory scenes were filmed in the enormous Innocenti factory, now completely abandoned and currently under consideration for possible housing in the very tight Milan market. Baxter and his colleagues all work Friden mechanical calculators, common machines in the insurance industry. The history of California-based Friden shares certain elements with Olivetti. After decades of producing typewriters and mechanical calculators, and after a triumph in the early '60s with its transistorized desktop calculator and then being taken over by Singer, the company folded in the 1970s, unable to compete with cheap Japanese technology for pocket calculators.

9. Perhaps Luciana would have used a standardized manual like one produced by Olivetti titled *Il calcolo meccanico nelle scuole commerciali: Istruzioni per l'uso delle macchine calcolatrici* (Fondo DCUS direzione communicazione ufficio stampa, ASO 241. 2156–2081 [2157], n.d. [1957?]). This manual offers instructions on how to position the hands and which fingers to use on which keys in order to "blind type" numbers into a calculator.

10. Adriano's speech, widely cited, is reproduced in *Notizie Olivetti*, no. 26 (April–May, 1955): 16.

11. The modernist glass building, known for its light, designed by Luigi Cosenza and others, opened in 1953. It still stands in Pozzuoli, near Naples. It currently houses a number of technology companies.

12. Ilva (later Italsider) was founded in 1910 in an area along the ocean near Pozzuoli. Its long history is fascinating. From early days, critics feared that the colossus would have damaging impacts on the environment surrounding its factories. In fact, at the time of this writing, there are ongoing lawsuits concerning the lethal effects of its activities, especially in the Puglia region.

13. Ettore Sottsass, "Disegno dei calcolatori elettronici," *Stile industria,* no. 20 (1959): 5–14, at 6. In 1964, Olivetti developed the world's first desktop or personal computer, the Programma 101. Like a mainframe, the Programma stored data on punch cards. In turn, these would be inserted into a slot while functions were performed on a keyboard, not dissimilar to a calculator, but programmable. The company sold about forty thousand units of the Programma 101 (primarily in the United States). Historians of the company reflect on the machine as being "ahead of its time."

14. While the Assassin, with his strong (exaggerated) southern accent, seems completely disjointed from the new technology, we eventually see that he actually has his own reel-to-reel tape player at home, in his "space-age bachelor pad." Perhaps this is not a crucial detail, since the treatment has him living instead in an apartment that once belonged to his parents, filled with heavy antique furniture. In the film, he is versed in high-resolution photography, perhaps even using a home dark room to develop his own set of images of staged murders involving his deceased lover. Ultimately, we should not expect *Investigation* to offer a coherent statement on technology. But, as one of the earliest Italian films featuring a mainframe, it has something to say about the relation of the computer to cinema itself by tying them up in a narrative about the police state.

7. Marriage on the Installment Plan

1. Kristin Ross calls the French couple, or *jeune ménage,* of the same period a significant social formation, a "newly vitalized unit of consumption energy" (Ross 1994, 59). She notes that their gender seems secondary to their dual power. They want the same things. They function as a unit, exemplified by Jérôme and Sylvie in George Perec's 1965 novel *Les choses.*

2. *The Refrigerator,* Monicelli's episode for the 1970 omnibus *Le coppie (The Couples),* finds actress Monica Vitti playing a wife who has a job in a retail store. Her husband gets by selling things on the street. They just need a small sum to keep the repo man from coming for their most prized possession, the refrigerator, the

most important domestic appliance, as discussed by Kristin Ross. So Vitti's character sells her body. Just once. The logic of this act (and the fact that it's a comedy) fits perfectly. No one is threatened, not even (apparently) her husband. But there are always more appliances to be had.

8. Dance Hall and Movie Theater

1. In its length, intensity, and vertiginous camera angles paralleling the drunken state of the partygoers, I have long suspected that this scene could be a possible homage to Federico Fellini's *carnevale* scene in his 1953 *I vitelloni*. In both cases, the party scene is the longest in the film, perhaps out of proportion to the narrative developments that come before (or after, in the case of *I vitelloni*). Paolo Villaggio seems to parody or at least metabolize both in the Christmas party in his first film of the Fantozzi series, *Fantozzi* (1975; directed by Luigi Salce). The rhythms of the evening accelerate because the leader of the orchestra—the Organizzazione Fellini—wants to go home sooner.

2. Ermanno Olmi, "Il drago da uccidere," interview by Ugo Casiraghi (of *L'unità*) and Morando Morandini (of *Milano-Sera*), *La fiera del cinema* 3, no. 11 (November 1961): 55–57.

3. The quote is from Siegfried Kracauer's essay "The Little Shopgirls Go to the Movies," (Kracauer 1995, 297). The fact that he is writing about the relation of cinema to daily life in 1930s Germany only reinforces the notion that boom Italy was (re)experiencing a set of social phenomena that had already been played out in more developed national cultures.

9. Night School

1. Archival material surrounding the film's genesis housed in the Biblioteca del Museo di Cinema, Turin, suggests that Petri and his cowriter, Ugo Pirro, had intended for a worker (perhaps the main character, perhaps someone else) to suffer an injury on the factory floor (a rather didactic gesture, in retrospect) to demonstrate the danger of the work and create sympathy. The surreal encounter with the psychiatrist was definitely added in

later, perhaps after some improvisation on set. In fact, for all that
the profession of the industrial shrink is parodied in this film,
Petri was fascinated by figures such as Reich. He took seriously
the idea that events occurring in the formation of individual subjectivity also repeat themselves in broader cultural and political
structures.

10. Milan Beach

1. Ponti married Loren (born Sofia Costanza Brigida Villani
Sciocolone) after obtaining a Mexican divorce from his first wife.
In 1960, just two years before the release of *Boccaccio '70,* the couple entered Italy and were called into court, where they denied
being married and subsequently had their marriage annulled. Several years later, Loren, Ponti, and his first wife moved to France, as
divorce was still illegal in Italy. In France, Ponti and Loren married
in a civil ceremony.

2. Yet it turns out not to be the case, so the couple marries out
of love and a desire for a household in the future, precisely on the
"layaway plan." In *Tempi stretti,* after agreeing to marry a man she
barely knows and does not love, Emma stays in the factory indefi-
nitely. In any case, the casual attitude toward the possible pregnancy does not seem to have preoccupied the censors and critics
of *Renzo and Luciana.* Reviews and the (rather scant) critical literature on the film, including Monicelli's own writings or responses to
interview questions, fail to mention what might be its most radical
element from a certain point of view. Put baldly, there is no interest
in the fetus.

11. Shifts

1. This is not the place to rehearse the larger argument about
artificial labor and enhanced domestic machinery from thinkers
such as Angela Davis, who pushed for women to leave the home to
avoid boredom and atomization, or Ellen Lupton, whose study of
the design of appliances concluded that they made women into individual consumers of products that they may have anthropomor-
phized, rather than producers of any sort of collective services.

Filmography

1926
Walter Ruttmann, *Acciaio* (*Steel*)

1928
King Vidor, *The Crowd*

1929
Corrado D'Errico, *Stramilano*

1944
Vittorio De Sica, *I bambini ci guardano* (*The Children Are Watching Us*)

1948
Vittorio De Sica, *Ladri di biciclette* (*Bicycle Thieves*)

1956
Ermanno Olmi, *Michelino 1° B*

1959
Gianni Puccini, *L'impiegato* (*The Office Worker*)

1960
Billy Wilder, *The Apartment*
Luchino Visconti, *Rocco e i suoi fratelli* (*Rocco and His Brothers*)
Nelo Risi, *Elea Classe 9000* (*Elea 9000 series—Olivetti documentary*)

1961
Michelangelo Antonioni, *La notte* (*The Night*)
Ermanno Olmi, *Il posto* (*The Job*)

1962
Alberto Lattuada, *Il mafioso*
Mario Monicelli, *Renzo e Luciana* (*Renzo and Luciana*; episode
from the omnibus *Boccaccio '70*)
Enzo Monachesi/Olivetti Corporation, *Arte programmata*
(*Programmed Art*; documentary)
Aristide Bosio/Olivetti Corporation, *Una macchina: un'officina*
(*A machine: a workshop*).

1963
Ugo Gregoretti, *Il pollo ruspante* (*Free Range Chicken*; episode
from the omnibus *RoGoPaG*)
Ugo Gregoretti, *Omicron*

1965
Antonio Pietrangeli, *Io la conoscevo bene* (*I Knew Her Well*)

1967
Dino Risi, *Il tigre* (*The Tiger and the Pussycat*)

1969
Ugo Gregoretti, *Apollon: una fabbrica occupata* (*Apollon: An
Occupied Factory*)

1970
Elio Petri, *Indagine di un cittadino al di sopra di ogni sospetto*
(*Investigation of a Citizen Above All Suspicion*)

1971
Elio Petri, *La classe operaia va in paradiso* (*The Working Class
Goes to Heaven*)

1995
Harun Farocki, *Arbeiter verlassen die Fabrik* (*Workers Leaving the
Factory*; video short)

2013
Michele Soavi, *Adriano Olivetti: La forza di un sogno* (*The Force
of a Dream*; television miniseries by RAI [*Radio Audizioni
Italiane,* called *Radiotelevisione italiana* since 1955; Italian
state television])

Bibliography

Alquati, Romano. (1962–63) 1975. "Composizione organica e forza-lavoro alla Olivetti." *Quaderni rossi*, no. 2 and no. 3. In *Sulla Fiat e altri scritti*, 83–163. Milan: Feltrinelli.

Aureli, Pier Vittorio. 2009. *The Project of Autonomy: Politics and Architecture within and against Capitalism*. New York: Buell Center and Princeton Architectural Press.

Beltrami, Ottorino. 1996. Interview by David Morton, July 30, 1996. Interview no. 286 for the IEEE History Center. Engineering and Technology History Wiki. ethw.org/Oral-History:Ottorino_Beltrami.

Ben-Ghiat, Ruth. 1995. "Fascism, Writing, and Memory: The Realist Aesthetic in Italy, 1930–1950," *Journal of Modern History* 67, no. 3 (September): 627–65.

Berardi, Franco (Bifo). 2002. *La fabbrica dell'infelicità*. Rome: DeriveApprodi.

Berardi, Franco (Bifo). 2009. *The Soul at Work*. Translated by Francesca Cadel and Giuseppina Mecchia. Preface by Jason Smith. Cambridge, Mass.: MIT Press.

Berta, Giuseppe. 2017. "L'idea di Olivetti e la riluttanza italiana." *Il sole 24 ore*, July 31, 2017. ilsole24ore.com/art/l-idea-olivetti-e-riluttanza-italiana-AEsJaa6B.

Bolognani, M. 2004. *Bit Generation: La fine della Olivetti e il declino dell'informatica italiana*. Introduction by M. Vitale. Rome: Editori Riuniti.

Bonomi, Aldo, Alberto Magnaghi, and Marco Revelli. 2015. *Il vento di Adriano. La comunità concreta di Olivetti tra non più e non ancora*. Rome: DeriveApprodi.

Brennan, AnnMarie. 2005. "Olivetti: A Work of Art in the Age of Immaterial Labour." *Journal of Design History* 28, no. 3: 235–53.

Bracco D., S. Della Casa, P. Manera, and F. Prono, eds. 2011. *Torino città del cinema*. Milan: Il Castoro.

Bricco, Paolo. 2014. *L'Olivetti dell'ingegnere*. Bologna: Il Mulino.

Carotti, Carlo. 1992. *Alla ricerca del paradiso: L'operaio nel cinema italiano 1945–1990*. Genoa: Graphos.

Casiraghi, Ugo, Morando Morandini, and Ermanno Olmi. 1961. "Il drago da uccidere." *La fiera del cinema* 3, no. 11 (November): 55–57.

De Certeau, Michel. 1984. *The Practice of Everyday Life*. Translated by Steven Rendell. Berkeley: University of California Press.

De Giorgi, Manolo, and Enrico Morteo, eds. 2008. *Olivetti: una bella società*. Turin: Umberto Allemandi.

De Landa, Manuel. 2000. *A Thousand Years of Nonlinear History*. New York: Swerve.

De Vincenti, Giorgio, ed. 2001. *Storia del cinema italiano*. Vol. 10, *1960–1964*. Venice: Marsilio.

Delvecchio, Raffaele. 2008. *La contrattazione aziendale: Esperienze in Olivetti 1975–1995*. Milan: Mondadori.

Di Carlo, Carlo, and Gaio Fratini, Eds. 1962. *Boccaccio '70*. Dal soggetto al film 22. Bologna: Cappelli.

Doray, Bernard. 1988. *From Taylorism to Fordism: A Rational Madness*. Translated by David Macey. London: Free Association Books.

Dyer-Witheford, Nick. 1999. *Cybermarx: Cycles and Circuits of Struggle in High Technology Capitalism*. Urbana: University of Illinois Press.

Farocki, Harun. 2002. "Workers Leaving the Factory." Translated by Laurent Faasch-Ibrahim. *Senses of Cinema* 21 (July). sensesofcinema.com/2002/harun-farocki/farocki_workers/.

Foot, John. 1999. "Cinema and the City: Milan and Luchino Visconti's Rocco." *Journal of Modern Italian Studies* 4, no. 2: 209–35.

Ford, Henry. 1926. *Today and Tomorrow*. Garden City, N.Y.: Doubleday.

Giacovelli, Enrico. 1990. *La commedia all'Italiana*. Rome: Gremese Editore.

Grande, Maurizio. 2003. *La commedia all'Italiana*. Edited by Orio Caldiron. Rome: Bulzoni.

Harwood, John. 2001. *The Interface: IBM and the Transformation of Corporate Design, 1945–1976.* Minneapolis: University of Minnesota Press.

Hester, Helen. 2017. "Promethean Labor and Domestic Realism." e-flux Architecture. e-flux.com/architecture/artificial-labor/140680/promethean-labors-and-domestic-realism/.

Kracauer, Siegfried. 1995. *The Mass Ornament: Weimar Essays.* Translated by Thomas Levin. Cambridge, Mass.: Harvard University Press.

Kracauer, Siegfried. 1998. *The Salaried Masses.* Translated by Quintin Hoare. London and New York: Verso.

La Rosa, Michele, Paolo A. Rebaudegno, and Chiara Ricciardelli, eds. 2004. *Storia e storie delle risorse umane in Olivetti.* Milan: FrancoAngeli.

Lekachman, Robert. 1966. *The Age of Keynes.* New York: Random House.

Markoff, John. 2005. *What the Dormouse Said: How the '60s Counterculture Shaped the Personal Computer Industry.* New York: Viking.

Mason, Paul. 2015. *Postcapitalism.* London: Allen Lane.

Meneguzzo, Marco, Enrico Morteo, and Alberto Saibene. 2012. *Programmare l'arte: Olivetti e le neoavanguardie cinetiche.* Milan: Johan and Levi.

Novara, Francesco, Renato Rozzi, and Roberta Garruccio, eds. 2005. *Uomini e lavoro alla Olivetti.* Milan: Mondadori.

Ottieri, Ottiero. 1957. *Tempi stretti.* Turin: Einaudi.

Ottieri, Ottiero. 1959. *Donnarumma all'assalto.* Milan: Bompiani.

Ottieri, Ottiero. 1963. *La linea gotica.* Milan: Bompiani.

Panzieri, Raniero. 1994. *Spontaneità e organizzazione: Gli anni dei "Quaderni Rossi" 1959–1964.* Edited by Stefano Merli. Pisa: Biblioteca Franco Serantini.

Pasquinelli, Matteo, ed. 2014. *Gli algoritmi del capitale: Accelerazionismo, macchine della conoscenza e autonomia del comune.* Verona: Ombre corte.

Pinkus, Karen. 1995. *Bodily Regimes: Italian Advertising under Fascism.* Minneapolis: University of Minnesota Press.

Pinkus, Karen. 2003. *The Montesi Scandal: The Death of Wilma*

Montesi and the Birth of the Paparazzi in Fellini's Rome. Chicago: University of Chicago Press.

Pinkus, Karen. 2017. "Disassembling the Drugged Machine." In *Vincenzo Agnetti: Territories*, 25–32. New York: Lévy-Gorvy Gallery.

Pirandello, Luigi. 1974. *Quaderni di Serafino Gubbio operatore*. Milan: Arnoldo Mondadori Editore. First published in 1916 as *Si gira! (Shoot)*, and then in 1925 with the full title.

Plotnick, Rachel. 2018. *Power Button: A History of the Pleasure, Panic, and Power of Pushing*. Cambridge, Mass.: MIT Press.

Pollock, Frederick. 1957. *Automation: A Study of its Economic and Social Consequences*. Translated by W. O. Henderson and W. H. Chaloner. New York: Praeger.

Rebaudegno, Paolo. 2016. *Olivetti: comunicazione, stile, design, architettura*. Pamphlet for Lezioni Olivettiane (Olivettian Lessons). Rome: Museo nazionale delle arti del XXI secolo (Fondazione MAXXI), May 20.

Revelli, Marco. 1989. *Lavorare in Fiat*. Milan: Garzanti.

Rhodes, John David. 2019. "D'errico's Stramilano." In *The City Symphony Phenomenon: Cinema, Art, and Urban Modernity Between the Wars*, edited by Steven Jacobs, Eva Hielscher, and Anthony Kinik, 96–105. New York: Routledge.

Rhodes, John David, and Elena Gorfinkel. 2011. *Taking Place: Location and the Moving Image*. Minneapolis: University of Minnesota Press.

Ross, Kristin. 1994. *Fast Cars, Clean Bodies*. Cambridge, Mass.: MIT Press.

Rushing, Robert. 2009. "De Sica's *The Children Are Watching Us*: Neorealist Cinema and Sexual Difference." *Studies in European Cinema* 6, no. 2–3: 97–111.

Sadler, Simon. 1998. *The Situationist City*. Cambridge, Mass.: MIT Press.

Seymour, Benedict. 2010. "Eliminating Labour: Aesthetic Economy in Harun Farocki." Mute, April 14, 2010. metamute.org/editorial/articles/eliminating-labour-aesthetic-economy-harun-farocki.

Schoonover, Karl. 2012. *Brutal Vision: The Neorealist Body in Postwar Italian Cinema*. Minneapolis: University of Minnesota Press.

Sottsass, Ettore. 1959. "Disegno dei calcolattori elettronici," *Stile Industria*, no. 20: 5–14.

Tobagi, Benedetta. 2008. *I volti e le mani*. DVD booklet to *Ermanno Olmi: Gli anni Edison. Documentari e cortometraggi: 1954–1958*. Milan: Feltrinelli.

Vercellone, Carlo. 1996. "The Anomaly and Exemplariness of the Italian Welfare State." Translated by Michael Hardt. In *Radical Thought in Italy*, edited by Michael Hardt and Paolo Virno, 81–98. Minneapolis: University of Minnesota Press.

Volponi, Paolo. 1962. *Memoriale*. Milan: Garzanti.

Volponi, Paolo. 1898. *Le mosche del capitale*. Turin: Einaudi.

Karen Pinkus is professor of Italian and comparative literature at Cornell University. She is the author of *Fuel: A Speculative Dictionary* (Minnesota, 2016) and *Bodily Regimes: Italian Advertising under Fascism* (Minnesota, 1995).